ASHLAND PSYCH MURDER

A Bridge Murder Series

Patricia Monroe Arnold

Pat Arnold

Ariel Publishing Company

San Francisco

Senior Editor: Morgan Rankin

Bridge Editors: Mark Hasey, Donnella Bloebaum
Computer Editor: Pam Benz

Library of Congress Cataloging-in-Publication

ISBN

Published by Ariel Publishing Company

Dedicated to my wonderful daughter, whose insights and great love of mysteries has inspired this book.

CHAPTER ONE

Inspector Grey picked up the phone on the first ring. A voice interrupted his solitude. "Do you know that there is a knife fight, two teenage suicides with illegal drugs involved going on in Ashland this very minute."

Suddenly alert in his chair, he barked loudly into the speaker. "Who is calling? What are you reporting?"

"I'm reporting the suicide of two teenagers happening right at this very minute." The woman's voice burned into his ear.

Grabbing a pencil, he pulled a memo pad squarely in front of him. "Where is this happening? Who is calling?" He pushed a button to bring up a trace.

"This is happening right now on the stage of the Angus Browmer Theater, here in Ashland."

Grey's face showed a slow burn as he sputtered, "Lady, that's not funny." But the line had gone dead.

•••••••••

Kitty Malone checked the speedometer again, trying hard to keep it under seventy five. It had been a little slower coming from Pacific Grove until they reached Highway 5; now it was straight sailing through the interior of the California Central Valley on to the Oregon border. Sarah Peters, her bridge partner and friend from Monterey, was fiddling with the radio dials, finally giving up and inserting a tape in the cassette player.

"This one should be good," she said, after looking through six or seven in the cassette box on the floor. "Great Duets in Italian Opera."

"One of my favorites," Kitty responded, as she lapsed into a reverie while the fields of Northern California skimmed past. She was glad that she had made this two week vacation possible for herself. Not that she had a regular job or was really on salary with the paper, but they expected a story every few weeks or so, along with the advertisements that, of necessity, went along with it. The Monterey Herald called her "an occasional writer", but she was expected to sell advertising to go with the story and that's how she made her commission. It allowed her the freedom, in the parlance of the small time entrepreneur, to make her own time.

She felt a rush of joi de vivre, relaxing her shoulders against the back of the seat, relishing the break in the routine of a well ordered life where her days were a methodical completion of daily tasks. In each day in her activities of work, bridge and community volunteerism, she planned something unique, so that there was nothing repetitive about her life.

Asking Sarah to come along to Ashland was a stroke of genius. She had become really friendly with her since they became partners in the New Monterey Duplicate Bridge Club. It was a new partnership, going well and now they were on a real vacation to see the plays and play bridge in beautiful Ashland.

"Shall we stop at the next rest stop, Sarah?" Kitty asked with a playful shake of her light brown hair, which framed a pleasant round face topping a slightly stout body.

She gave the impression of a typical tourist but underneath her jolly exterior was a very determined person. Shyness or uncertainty was a concept that never entered her head. In her work selling advertising, she never waited in line in a store but went right up to inquire for the "big boss". She was polite so that nobody seemed to mind her intrusion, though she often thought that a man might not get away with such forwardness.

Kitty had picked Sarah up around eight o'clock, and they had only eaten egg salad sandwiches that she made the night before. The first of the handy rest stops on US 5 was coming up in a few miles.

"Good idea. We need to stretch our legs and take a break."

Kitty pulled into the green oasis in the middle of the played out yellow fields of varied crops that covered the landscape. Cotton, pushing through the dark brown pods, was an interesting crop in this rich agricultural area, but it had been mostly plucked and the fields were a mashed brown with a residue of bright white spots where the machines had wasted the crop.

Kitty took a traditional red checkered table cloth and wicker picnic basket from the car as Sarah headed for the cement and stone rest rooms, her tall, lithe body moving smoothly on the tree shaded lawn. She was close to fifty, worked as a substitute teacher during the year, but took off every summer, divorced for many years with no children. She had short brown hair and a sharp, wise face.

The area was spotted with stone picnic tables and the partners quickly found a vacant one. After Kitty spread out a fruit salad from the ice chest and different drinks, salsa and chips, she took her turn at the rest room. When they had settled down for a quick repast, she pulled out the tickets and the schedule for the Oregon Shakespeare Festival.

"Tonight the theaters are dark, as always on Monday, so our first program is tomorrow evening at the Bowmer,*Romeo and Juliet.* We can go to the bridge club that afternoon and see how we do with the theatrical types of Ashland and Medford county."

"Is it a big club or small like our Monterey club?" Sarah asked.

"The space is actually bigger, conveniently located on the road to Lithia Park, but I don't know how many people come to play. I never even noticed it for the years that Peter and I used to go to Ashland. Last year with Elder Hostel I just peeked in because they kept us so busy with all the plays and lectures. I never had time to play bridge. It looked like a goodly number, at least a dozen tables."

Kitty had been widowed for five years but her husband had never played duplicate bridge. Now she played at least twice a week. They had come to Ashland for the plays for many years before his illness and death. This vacation would give her time to play bridge often during the day since they had tickets to all the plays, mostly in the evenings–three in the outdoor Elizabethan Theater, three in the Bowmer and two plays at the exclusive intimate Black Swan Theater. It was always hard to get tickets for the theater-in-the-round at the Black Swan, but Kitty had sent in a donation and received an early program. She and Sarah had talked about going and the best date, so she sent for the tickets almost as soon as the program arrived last October. Now they were on their way in the middle of June with tickets to eight plays spaced out over two weeks. She couldn't imagine that this pleasant vacation would result in her becoming completely immersed in a murder laced with sex, lust and revenge.

Kitty had taken the first shift driving so now, with Sarah at the wheel, she noticed that the fields were getting greener after miles of apricot trees (green but without signs of fruit yet) as they left the cut-off to Sacramento. It was a little hard to recognize at first; then Kitty slowly realized that the fields were covered in rice. She could even see the water at the bottom under the green sticks closer to the road.

"This must be irrigated by the Sacramento River," Kitty said knowingly. She turned to Sarah admiring her soft brown hair falling around her face. Her sharp, attractive features were relaxed and she looked younger than her fifty years. Kitty herself was sixty-three, but when you pass forty, age between friends doesn't matter at all,she mused. Kitty wore her years well since she dyed her hair ash blond. She tried lacklusterly to diet but wavered between 145 and 150, always remaining about ten pounds heavier than the charts said she should be.

"I've been noticing the rice. The posters at the rest stop told a lot about Sacramento's rice. Fifty percent of the country's rice is produced here," Sarah stated with authority.

"It's really beautiful," Kitty answered. "You can see all the rice processing plants. See, there's one coming up."

They passed an ugly industrial building, metal, painted white with four conical bins, pipes and metal towers.

"The posters said that rice was introduced by the Chinese in the 1900's with small plots, but now they flood the fields and seed by plane. It's a marvelous preserve for waterfowl and more than one third of the water is recycled."

Kitty marveled at this information from her friend. She'd never taken much notice of the rest stop wooden information stand covered by the shake roof, except to glance at a map showing where they were.

Ahead Mount Shasta was now in her vision. Looking incredibly majestic, even so many miles away, it loomed large in her sights, one of the vistas that make this part of California so remarkable.

"We'll be coming to Mt. Shasta soon, Sarah, and Lake Shasta."

Sarah dutifully exclaimed at the size of the mountain ahead. The other mountains were craggy peaks but nothing compared to Shasta with its top covered in snow, even in late June.

"Is that snow, that white stuff on top," Sarah asked childishly.

Kitty laughed. "Yes, it's 20,000 feet, but we won't come to it for a little while. The Rouge River is way down to your right."

They stopped again in Shasta City for some coffee and tea and a little rest.

"It doesn't look as impressive up close as it did on the highway driving toward it," Sarah commented. "Of course you can't even see the top."

They changed places again and when they passed Shasta Dam Lake, Sarah was hanging out the window.

"It looks like it's in a terra cotta bathtub," Sarah exclaimed. "It's pretty low at this time of year," Kitty replied, "but there's a lot of it."

With every turn of the road another finger of the lake jutted out toward them.

"Aren't those darling little boats."

"Yes, the houseboats rent by the week, with a kitchen and plenty of bedrooms. They're really much bigger than they look from here."

"What a great way for a family to spend a vacation."

After the steep but gorgeous grades of the Siskiyou Mountains following the Shasta River, where it splashed down into the tranquil Shasta Dam Lake, it was refreshing to take the long grade down into the Rogue River Valley. The exit for Ashland was almost the first stop. They pulled off at Main Street, passed the Town Square and drove two blocks more to their two-story bed and breakfast, The Hathaway Arms. Driving up the steep concrete to the parking in the back, they gratefully opened the door and stretched their legs. The hill where the charming two-story white Victorian was perched provided an intimate view of the town of Ashland. The main street crossed a wide bridge over a full roiling creek that led past restaurants and small buildings to a triangular grouping of two story buildings and diagonal parking. Up a slight slope they could see the Shakespeare Center. Only the large corner building and the back of the Bowmer Theater was visible from their vantage point. Beyond, perhaps one or two blocks, was the tallest building on the landscape, rising seven stories in all its art deco glory, the Mark Anthony Hotel.

"We can easily walk to everything from this place," Kitty observed. "It looks very nice and clean. I can't wait to take a bath and get a good night's sleep."

"This is a great view. What's that tall building?"

"That's the Mark Anthony Hotel, though I think it's been sold recently. I stayed there once with John–very noisy because we were right over the bar. It's on the National Registry of Historic Places, as quite a few old houses are here. Are you as hungry as I am?"

" I am," Sarah confessed. "Maybe we could get a little late night dinner or a snack."

"Good idea. The bath and sleep can wait for that."

They rang the bell after pulling their main luggage out of the car. The grey haired, plump woman who answered the door was pleased to see them and showed them to rooms on the second floor.

"We'll get our exercise with all the hills and steps," Sarah observed, but Kitty was busy looking at the wine and cheese tray. "What a nice idea to have this ready for us. Thank you very much." The gentle, matronly house-keeper merely smiled and gave them both a key to the front door.

"Be sure to lock the door. There are a lot of ruffians hanging out at the Town Square these days. I'm Mrs. Williams and I'm here most mornings and Sunday and Monday evenings."

"Are you the owner to whom I spoke to when I made our reservation?" Kitty asked.

"I'm Jane Adam's good friend. She's the owner, and I help her when I can."

"Well, thank you for helping us. Are there any restaurants still open past eight o'clock?"

"I have some hot muffins I just made for breakfast, if that will do you."

"Oh, thank you, Mrs. Williams, but we need to stretch

our legs and look around a bit. We'll look forward to them for breakfast, though."

"Of course. There are plenty of places on the Square that are open all hours. Well, good night, " and she slipped out the door.

"Let's take a look at this notorious Town Square," laughed Sarah as she nibbled some cheese while downing a small glass of sherry.

●●●●●●●●●●

Juanita moved over a few inches so that another person, dressed in a grey-brown homespun garment that touched the ground, enveloping the body and giving no indication of the gender of this androgenous person, could sit beside her on the bench.

"Hey, B.J." she said, pointing her coke can toward the West. "Isn't the twilight a beautiful time? So purple, so still. You can't even hear the trumpet from the grand stage on a night like this."

"That's because it's Monday. It's dark," B.J. answered, taking out a crushed cigarette.

Juanita West pulled her bare feet under her long Indian batik dress , and hummed as she looked at the birds circling in the tall trees, heading home to their nests.

"This is the most peaceful time of the day. I could sit here all night, maybe I will, too."

Her mother was an artist, living in a barnlike structure out on the north end of town, who never worried about where she was. Juanita was fifteen now and quite able to take care of herself. She could take the bus or hitch a ride home or stay in town all night if she felt like it, though mostly she got tired around eleven or twelve o'clock. Summer was great, and she didn't have to get up early for school or anything. She'd never had a job and there was always something to eat at home or from her friends.

" B.J, you can see the moon through those large pines. Isn't that cool?" she asked her older friend.

"A wonderful part of the universe, right here in our backyard." B.J. commented.

Juanita tucked her legs under her in a lotus position and reached under the bench for her guitar. She strummed some chords and, humming first, started a little song about the moon, making up words that sounded like her mood. Looking across the square, she saw a young man starring at her. He was slight but well built. His hair was dark but his face was in the light so she could discern his handsomely chiseled features.

She looked away but knew he was watching her, and she changed her words to blue eyes in the purple night. He was coming right to her, she could see, but didn't want to acknowledge him since she'd never seen him before, not a regular in the Summer Town Square group.   He moved right in front of her and squatted on his heels. He was very good looking, she could see, as she looked up at the trees and the town arch and changed her tune to one more familiar to anyone with a radio.

"You are the most beautiful thing I have ever seen." His ardor was infectious, and she looked down at him and smiled. The light of her eyes burned right into his and they didn't say a word, just looked at each other.

"Will you walk with me?" He put out his hand and she

Page 10

slipped from her yoga position to stand next to him on the pavement. She came up to his chin. With his arm linked around her waist, she moved off toward Lithia Park walking closely beside him.

"Look out for my guitar, B.J.," she called back over her shoulder.

•••••••••

Kitty and Sarah came out of a barbecue restaurant, each toting a large roll and lots of beef. They walked toward the square, which was a small rectangle with diagonal parking on all sides. There was a brick rotunda in the center and rows of drinking fountains on each side. The ones closest to them were pitted with corrosive green metal and those opposite, fewer in number, looked pretty regular. There were just a few young people lounging around on benches .

"They don't look like desperados to me," Kitty said, glancing at the interestingly dressed group.

"You might get a kick out of the Lithia water fountains. I can't stand the stuff myself, but it's supposed to be good for you."

Sarah went over to the fountain and took a small taste. "It's not bad–pretty strong, very medicinal." She took a bigger swallow, then spit it out. "It's too strong for me."

"Come through this lawn area to the steps behind the Shakespeare theater complex," Kitty said as she led Sarah across the street and through the delicately landscaped lawn to the wide back steps going up to the Bowmer Theater. They passed young lovers lying on the grass, under the ornamental pines and ash trees, as they oohed and aahed at the gorgeously planted flowers on each side of the steps going up to the courtyard.

Kitty was always amazed at the beautiful landscaping throughout the whole properties of the Oregon Shakespeare Festival. She'd never seen a weed or dead plant. At home, her vegetable garden was always full of grass (weeds) and, ironically, in the small lawn in front of her home, the grass was sparse.

They passed the backs of restaurants and the Tudor Gift Shop across from the largest indoor theater, named for Angus Bowmer, the founder of the Shakespeare experience in Ashland almost fifty years ago. In the center of a sloping lawn on three sides was a raised stage.

"This is the Green where they have shows every night before the performances in the Elizabethan theater in the summer. It's a free show and very well done–music and dance. Pretty much of the period and lately they do interpretive dancing around the theme of the play that night. You'll love it."

It was very quiet, hardly any people this night since all the theatres were dark. They went back down the broad steps into the corner of Lithia Park. The night was light with a bright moon so they walked up to the duck pond passing hardly anyone, noticing only a few lovers kissing on the benches or stretched out under the trees.

"What a romantic setting for lovers," Kitty exclaimed. "Better go get our beauty sleep so we'll be ready for our big day tomorrow."

"First bridge then *Romeo and Juliet* tomorrow night, right?" Sarah asked.

"Right," Kitty replied as they walked quickly and de-terminedly across the lawn of the park, jaywalked across Main St. and then up the sidewalk to their handsome bed and breakfast.

••••••••••

Tuesday morning was always a big day for Janet. She hung the three green banners with the fleur de lis and a picture of the Bard on the posts in front of her tiny yard. It made her happy to transform the little house she had bought a year ago with a good portion of her savings. Located on the side street, only three blocks from the Shakespearian Center, she considered herself fortunate to have found such a conveniently located house, tiny as it was, to pursue her life-long dream of being part of the center of the Shakespearian milieu in Ashland. Janet Millhouse had written a book, two volumes in fact, on Shakespeare. It was her joy and her obsession. It was never published because she didn't have the academic credentials, the publishers said. She'd given up after sub-mitting it to four different companies . After years of dreams and plans, she decided to move to Ashland so that she could open a museum featuring her art work and Shakespeare memorabilia. She made plans to give lec-tures on the productions at the two Shakespearian the-aters.

It was a big gamble, she knew, since it had taken months last year to find a house close enough to the the-atres and within her meager price range. There was a shed in the back of the narrow lot where she had set up her printmaking apparatus. It was too cold in the winter but quite functional in the warm weather. She had opened up the living and diningrooms and kitchen so that there was now one large room, at least enough for fifteen people. She had enclosed the kitchen appliances behind a carved wooden screen and decorated the walls with more of her silk screen banners and some of her prints, attractively colored by her friend, Wanda West.

It was a wise decision to concentrate on the printmaking and silkscreening which, along with her daily lectures at 11 am, 2 pm and 4, made for a busy week. It was very difficult during the winter, but in spring and now the busy summer season, it looked like she might be able to make a living.

Wanda was her first and so far only friend in Ashland, and she had given her the job to paint a few of her cards and small prints. When she found that those were the ones that sold to the play goers that trickled by her Museum, she continued the practice. She could never attain the bright happy colors that Wanda used, even though she tried. Her designs and colors were much more Elizabethan, more in tone with the dark Merlin-like robe that she wore for her lectures.

She looked out the window to see two middle aged couples coming up the walk, printed brochure in hand, She went to the door, opening it with a welcoming smile, thinking again how wise it was to make a brochure to place in all the racks in the center of town.

"Is this the place for the Museum and lecture?" one of the grey-haired men asked.

"Yes, come right in. This is the Shakespearian Museum and Art Gallery." And she swung the door open.

"The lectures are two dollars per person, but won't start until 11 am. You may look at the Gallery and decide if you want to stay for the lecture."

She chatted with them, showing her artifacts on the Bard, painstakingly collected over the years. An antique reproduction of the 1623 folio, her pride and joy, rested under glass near the front of the room. Two more couples arrived at the door and told her they had heard about her fine lectures from a friend who had been there a few weeks ago. Eight people was pretty good for a morning talk, she thought, as she brought out chairs for all and stepped to the front of the room.

"Yesterday I called the Ashland police station to report a stabbing and suicide of teenagers involving the use of illegal drugs. I told them it was happening right here in Ashland on the stage of the Bowmer Theater." Her blue eyes twinkled in her round face framed by salt and pepper black hair, loosely pulled into a knot at the back of her head.

Her audience laughed appropriately and knowingly, as she launched into the details of her analysis of *Romeo and Juliet*, with the startling announcement that Friar Lawrence had been a jilted lover of Juliet's mother who wanted to get back at his former love.

"He conspired with *the pair of star-cross'd lovers* against the Capulets," she said and explained further that since he never conscientiously informed Romeo that Juliet was only in a drug-induced deathlike state, not really dead, there must have been some reason. Giving the letter to the bumbling Friar John, who gave a lame excuse and returned home with the undelivered letter could only have been done maliciously. This theory was delivered with enthusiastic certainty.

Janet always had to find the deeper reason within the text of Shakespeare. She studied the text like a bible and tried to find a reason for every little nuance or action. She was aware of the arguments among Shakespearian scholars regarding their difference between the 1604 Quarto and the Folio that she used for all her studies.

Her audience was quite intrigued with her theory on the tragedy of the two lovers and argued a bit with her about the Friar Lawrence theory. They ended up buying a large number of the colored cards that were suitable for framing, as Janet herself so often announced.

I'll have to call Wanda for more, she thought. Since the ones I have may not last out the week, maybe Juanita can deliver them when she comes to Ashland from her barn studio north of town. With that thought, she said good-bye to her visitors and slipped behind the screen of her kitchen to make herself a quick sandwich.

CHAPTER TWO

Kitty and Sarah opened the screen door of the Ashland Bridge Club on the street adjacent to Lithia Park. It was a large room with ten tables set up, coffee pot area and bathrooms at the rear. It looked cheerful with light walls and a natural pine wood floor. There were a number of people already at tables, as the two newcomers went over to the computer desk. The florid, fiftyish man was dealing out a deck of cards and setting them into the four sections of the card holders.

"Hello. We're Kitty Malone and Sarah Peters. I called from Monterey so that we could play bridge."

" Oh, yes, I'm John Figler. I'm the one you talked to. All duplicate players are welcome any time. Do you want to give me your ACBL numbers so I can put them in the computer?"

The American Contract Bridge League, to which most of them belonged, promoted the spirit of goodwill and friendliness but with such a competitive game, points were very important.

After giving him their numbers, Kitty and Sarah helped themselves to some coffee, tea in the case of Kitty, and asked at one of the tables if the East/West positions were open.

"Yes, it's open. There's no one here. You're welcome." The women from Monterey introduced themselves to a small man, with a thin mustach, named Larry and his rather stout partner, Tim. They all picked up the hands that John had placed before them. The first hand was definitely North/South's and Kitty and Sarah did the best they could to defend and kept it to four spades bid and made.

On the second hand North bid one spade, and Kitty, sitting to his right and with four spades in her hand and about twelve points, passed. If they went on in spades, we might score on penalties, she thought. South passed and Sarah bid two hearts. North passed and Kitty bid two no-trump since she only had two hearts. A pass to Sarah who bid three hearts, and it was passed out. When the dummy was laid out, Sarah was surprised to see the four spades and a very good hand.

Here are the hands:

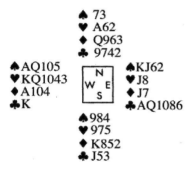

```
                 ♠ 73
                 ♥ A62
                 ♦ Q963
                 ♣ 9742
  ♠ AQ105                    ♠ KJ62
  ♥ KQ1043      ┌───────┐    ♥ J8
  ♦ A104        │  N    │    ♦ J7
  ♣ K           │ W   E │    ♣ AQ1086
                │   S   │
                └───────┘
                 ♠ 984
                 ♥ 975
                 ♦ K852
                 ♣ J53
```

"Why did you bid a spade?" Sarah turned to North, "You only had two little ones."

"It was a psych," he answered diffidently, his small beady eyes staring defiantly at her. A "psych" is a bridge term for a false bid that fools the opponents and the partner as well.

They made five hearts, but most of the players in the room had bid six spades or six no-trump. After one more hand, they left the table to play with the next couple. Sarah was a little upset.

"We never have any psychs at our club, that I can remember," she told Kitty as they walked to the new table.

"I don't ever remember it happening in the club, either, but it's perfectly legal. We can't call the director or anything. We just better watch out for that here. Maybe it's a tone of this club."

The next two tables were pretty regular, and Kitty and Sarah held their own in the middle range of scores. Each score was noted on a slip of paper, called the traveler, that was then placed on the back of the boards. There were twenty seven boards that day and all the tables played the same hands. The fun, competitive part came when you judged your score against the others. Kitty and Sarah were happy to stay in the middle after the bad board at the first table.

At the next table, our newcomers to Ashland bridge met the most formidable lady in the city, both in bridge and in other affairs of the community, especially the board of the Oregon Shakespearian Festival.

They sat down, smiled and Kitty announced. "Hello. We're Kitty and Sarah from Monterey."

"Yes, I heard your names announced by John at the beginning of play. Are you staying long?" spoken in a tone of disinterest from a thin aristocratic looking woman. She was in her mid-forties, very blond with her hair coiffured in a chignon, attractively dressed in a well-tailored suit with rings on four of her fingers. "I'm Stella and this is my son, Brian."

The girls turned to stare into the deep blue eyes of a very attractive young man who was probably about nineteen or twenty.

"Glad to meet you. I hope you don't psych like some of the other players."

"Oh, that's standard practice here. You can look at my card if you wish," Stella said haughtily, holding out her convention card.

"If you're not ready to compete, don't enter the game."

Kitty and Sarah were very quiet during the rest of the play, but they noticed that Stella held a heavy hand over her son, talking to him sharply at the end of the game when he hadn't supported her suit and she made game. She was more aggressive in her bidding, so that she ended up playing most of the hands. The Monterey pair played one hand, in spite of a strange bid by Stella, just bidding their own count and not letting the opponents interfere. They bid and made three no-trump, which was near the top score because a number of others were in three spades making three.

John announced there would be a five minute break before moving to the next table.

Kitty and Sarah filled up on more tea and coffee. When they returned to the table, Kitty complimented Stella on her beautiful suit and asked if she had lived in Ashland for a long time. Stella, much friendlier after the compliment, explained that they had been coming up from Los Angeles for a number of years before they decided to move here.

"My husband's a screen writer, so he can work anywhere. We fell in love with a large Victorian in the hills with a view of the entire valley."

"How wonderful for you. You're also lucky that your son will play bridge with you. Most children stay as far as possible from their parents at that age," Sarah offered, a knowlegeable teacher of high school students.

"Brian's a great player," Stella said with a slight frown at the concept brought up by Sarah.

Brian, aroused from a reverie by the mention of his name, exclaimed,

"I'm in love. I'm in love." He looked around him as if realizing where he was. " With bridge," he added, in a warm, soft tone of voice and a charming laugh.

Stella looked sharply at her son, then smiled

"He's a romantic about everything. This was his first year at college here in Ashland, and he became the school poet. Quite a few pieces were published." It was hard to discern whether she was disdainful or admiring from her tone. Probably a little of both, Kitty decided as she and Sarah rose to resume the play at the next table.

"It was very nice talking to you, Stella. What's your last name?" Kitty asked

"Jacobs. My husband is Oscar Jacobs."

"Oh, yes," Kitty replied meaningfully, as if she had heard of him, which she had not.

At the next table, Marge and Joy introduced themselvs to the newcomers. They were long-time players at the club, polite but very competitive. On the second hand, Kitty and Sarah liked their cards and bid game in spades. The opponents bid five diamonds and neither Kitty nor Sarah felt they had the point count to bid five spades, and passed. North only made four diamonds–down one. The other tables either bid four and made it or doubled five diamonds. "I'm sorry I didn't double, partner," Kitty said.

"I should have doubled," Sarah said. "I had three diamonds to the jack."

As they left the club on their way to Main Street, Kitty said, "It makes you appreciate your own club, doesn't it."

"There's something spooky about that place, Kitty," Sarah replied. "Do we really want to go back tomorrow?"

"Maybe there will be different people there next time," Kitty said hopefully.

They stopped by a deli that looked out over the River. Walking up the wooden stairs in the back, they were seated on the balcony overlooking the roaring waters below. With such an extensive menu, they had a hard time deciding on a brown rice and veggie meal, which was delicious. They walked up the hill in a determined manner, back to their rooms so that they could dress for the evening and *Romeo and Juliet* at the Bowmer.

•••••••••

They joined the crowd in front of the theater where a curved semi-circular grassy slope looked down on the oblong stage. There were eight musicians in Elizabethan robes playing a variety of instruments.

"Oh, the green show has already begun!" Kitty exclaimed as she led the way, climbing over people's knees to a small patch of unoccupied grass. "This will give us a good view." She settled Sarah next to her in the cramped quarters. "Next time we'll come earlier."

Five acrobatic dancers appeared, in flowing exotic chiffon for the three women, and blue tights for the two men. Then another man appeared in kingly robes and leapt to the middle of the stage. They followed a choreographed script that highlighted the concepts of The Winter's Tale that was showing that night at the outdoor Elizabethan theater. Kitty had bought tickets for that play for the Friday performance The audience was deeply appreciative and their applause resounded at the end of each of the three performances.

"Wow, what a treat. It would be worth coming here just to see that!" Sarah exclaimed. They followed the crowd that was moving into the circular glass door of the Angus Bowmer Theater.

Kitty and Sarah settled themselves into center seats K 3-4 half way up the rows that looked down in a semicircle on the sparsely decorated stage. They were soon enthralled by Elizabethan language coming from an energetic cast dressed in black leather, for all the world like two Italian or New York street gangs.

"I'm not sure I appreciate the modern dress. I'm really not used to it," Sarah told Kitty as they moved to the lobby during intermission.

"They do it all the time here. I think it makes the play more vital. But they never change the words. Cut some, once in a while, but the action is what makes the play as well as the words. The words are so wonderful, you almost feel like talking that way, *Sirrah,*" she added with a laugh for the pun on the ubiquituous salutary title in

Shakespeare's plays.

"Come look at this cute display of dolls dressed in the fashion of so many years." They descended the landing to the restroom entrance and admired the fashion display of hundreds of years of women's clothing.

On the way out of the theater, they stopped to admire the plantings in front of the Bowmer. Kitty bent down and said *"That which we call a rose by any other name would smell as sweet."*

"Good one, Kitty. But we should leave now. *Good night, good night. Parting is such sweet sorrow that I shall say good night till it be morrow.* Not quite appropriate, I'm afraid."

"Good enough," complimented Kitty.

•••••••••

Janet was picking up the teacups from the last group of customers when there was a light knock on the door. She always served tea at the last lecture since it was generally close to four and she loved the English habit of "tea with simple pastries". She only charged a dollar more for the last session and though there was nothing expensive in the way of pastry, the customers always loved it, and bought more cards and prints than they did in the other sessions. As she turned from the hidden kitchen galley, she saw Wanda coming in the door. How prompt, she thought, since she had only asked her for more cards yesterday.

"Wanda, you're a dear. I didn't expect you to bring

them to me the next day!"

The attractive young woman, who was already coming through the door, was in her mid thirties, hazel eyes, clear and compassionate looking, tall, with long brown hair hanging loosely around her face.

"I was up quite late last night waiting for Juanita to come home, so I kept myself busy." She laid down the box of cards and took a seat on the sofa by the window. She was dressed in a light summer Indian madras in tones of blue which went well with her blue eyes and fair skin.

"She thinks I don't worry about her, but I can never get to sleep until she gets home. I give her complete freedom because I love and trust her so much, and I want the ties to be as loose as gossamer strands," she laughed at the Shakespearean metaphor. They always seemed to come out when she was with Janet, the Elizabethan lady.

"Well, you wouldn't want her to have a baby like you did at seventeen." Janet was a trifle old-fashioned in these matters. Of course she had had sons but she was always very strict with them.

Wanda, blushing slightly, hastened to assure her good friend, "You know it was my strict upbringing that made me revolt and become pregnant so that I could become an independent adult."

She had moved out of her home in Los Angeles and survived on welfare when Juanita was a baby. The baby's father was in and out of their lives but never in a marital *menage.* She had pursued her artistic inclination and sold a few decorative pieces to galleries that were more like boutiques in the beach towns. Four years ago she had followed some friends who were also artists to Ashland and had fallen in love with the atmosphere and ambiance. She rented a place just outside of town with small living quarters attached to the barn she used as a studio. She was able to make a small living with her paintings placed on consignment in an Ashland gallery, and she had done one large mural for a coffee shop in town. Roberto had sent some child support from time to time, and she was pleased that she was now off welfare and more independent.

"These are beautiful, Wanda. You are very talented." Janet smiled broadly. "Of course you could paint your own cards and do very well without using my printed designs as a background though I shouldn't tell you that because I might lose you."

"You won't lose me, Janet. Besides it's fun and I can do it without thinking while I watch the sunset or talk to friends. If I had to make up my own, as when I paint, it would take enormous thought and energy. You're stuck with me for a while. Here's my bill." And she passed over a folded sheet of paper.

"I've had a very good two days this week, six or eight sales at every lecture, mostly on *Romeo and Juliet*. One couple wanted to come back for *The Winter's Tale* lecture, so I shifted to that this afternoon. See how many cards I've sold," Janet said, pointing to the racks at the front of the room.

"That's great. I'll go to work on the next batch if you have enough printed. You know Juanita came back last night floating on cloud nine. She says she's in love with a beautiful boy. I'm surprised she had never met him before, but he probably didn't move in the same circles even in this small town."

"Who is it?" Janet asked expectantly.

"Well, my darling Juanita has fallen in love with Brian Jacobs, the son of Mrs. High and Mighty Stella Jacobs."

Just at that moment they heard the doorbell ring and, staring at the open entrance, saw two women at the front door that had been left ajar when Wanda came in.

"I hope we're not disturbing you, but we heard from friends in Monterey that this was an interesting museum. Is it open?" Kitty Malone and Sarah Peters were smiling but a little disconcerted because they had just overheard the previous conversation in the small confines of the reconverted house.

"Yes, we stay open until 5:30, but most of the day is taken up with lectures. Here is the schedule." Janet gave her a printed form and sensing the friendly tentative stance of her visitors, said graciously, "You are welcome to come in and view my small but unique museum to the Bard right here in the heart of the city devoted to his work. I'm Janet Millhouse We were just restocking some of our beautiful cards."

She went to the racks with the box that Wanda had brought and began filling in the empty spaces.

Kitty and Sarah were charmed by the cards. Rustic, heavy tan paper gave an old English look to the attractive designs of lads and damsels in Elizabethan dress, fools and kings as well as pictures of the great Shakespeare himself. Each card was about six by six inches and colored in subtle but attractive colors. "How much are they?" Sarah asked.

"They are ten dollars each, suitable for framing, each one individually painted by my dear friend, Wanda West."

Kitty and Sarah looked through the card case and at the

larger pictures that hung on the wall as Janet returned to her seat beside Wanda and resumed her conversation in lower tones.

"He is a pretty lad, must be all of eighteen, but not one to stand on his own two feet. *O Spirit of love, how quick and fresh art thou.* Isn't he just a freshman at Oregon State? Does the Queen know yet?"

"He finished his first year, according to Juanita, and it's too early to tell anyone. They've just met, and you know how young love is, it might blow over tomorrow."

In the small room, Kitty turned to Janet saying, "I couldn't help but overhear. We played bridge with Stella and Brian Jacobs yesterday and again today. He seems like a charming boy, very bright and very handsome."

"Oh, so you played with Mrs. Gotrocks, eh? Hope you survived with your skin intact."

"Now, Janet, don't be so harsh," Wanda interjected, "I'm sure Stella has some good qualities. Maybe she's nice at bridge."

"She's a good bridge player but about as warm as a salamander," Kitty replied. "She does lay a heavy trip on her boy. We could tell that in just a few encounters. I guess she's not a friend of yours, Janet?"

"There are plenty in town that are cowed by her as well. She's chair of the Benefactors Committee and on the Board of the Oregon Shakespeare Festival. She damn near runs everything in town."

"Now, Janet. She's not that important, just carries a big stick because she gives a lot of money to the Festival. You know they could never make it on subscription sales alone." She turned to explain to Kitty and Sarah, "But Stella Jacobs has made it next to impossible for Janet to be recognized for her true value in this town."

"She seems to hate me, puts down everything I do. I had hoped
to get involved with the Festival, but they have turned a cold shoulder to me. Everything I've done is on my own. They won't include me in anything they print, act like I don't exist, actually. I think it's mostly Queen Stella's fault."

Kitty nodded symphatetically. "I'm sorry to hear that. You should get recognition in town. Maybe it's too early I know thay everything takes time here. I used to come often wih my late husband. This is a charming place and your art work is quite beautiful. We would like to buy some cards now and we'll come back for one of your lectures, maybe tomorrow. Would that be all right?"

"It will be on *Romeo and Juliet* tomorrow. Have you seen it yet?"

"It was great, though it's hard for me to get used to the modern dress," Sarah commented.

"Well, come tomorrow at 11 o'clock if you're free." She took the cards they held, put them in a bag and gave change from a small drawer in the desk near the door.

"Thank you. We'll see you tomorrow."

They left the small building and made their way toward the main street to stop by the Welcome Center and look at last year's costume display.

This unique building was located at the corner of Main and Pioneer streets, at the bottom of the hill that led to the outdoor theater and the Green. The large store style windows were decorated with scenes from last year's plays. Mannikins in heavy Elizabethan gowns and a Victorian corner with a realistic feast set on the table were part of the charming display. The Welcome Center was part of the complex attached to the Tudor Guild, a bustling gift shop with two levels of tee shirts, coffee mugs, and Shakespearean texts. The merchandise was stylized and charming, fools heads competing with appropriate tapes and CDs.

"They even let you try on some of the most fabulous garments
so that you can be photographed as a queen or a knave."

"That would be fun. When can we do it?"

Tomorrow morning, before we go to the 11 o'clock lecture."

"Thank you. We'll see you tomorrow," Kitty told the volunteer sitting at the small desk at the door.

"Do you want to eat now, Sarah? Or shall we go back and get changed for the outdoor theater tonight. It gets really cold in the Elizabethan theater late at night. Hopefully it won't rain."

"Yes. Let's go back and change or at least get a sweater. I got a little chilly just walking home from the Bowmer last night. What happens if it rains? Do they go on with the show outdoors?"

"It only rains after midnight, like Camelot. That's why all the gardens are so beautiful. But seriously, the rain comes and goes. If it's very heavy, they change out of their costumes so those can be protected and go on with the show in street clothes and jeans.

As they passed the Ashland Bakery, they noticed a young man coming out of the store with a bag in his hand. Moving with a confident swing to his body, he seemed oblivious to the sideways glances that were sent his way.

"I think that was one of the actors we saw last night in *Romeo and Juliet*. Doesn't he look like the one ...Oh, what was his name?" Sarah whispered to Kitty.

"Yes, he does look very familiar. They all live around here so it's not unusual to see them in the markets or on the streets. It's a great life for the actors here because most of them work almost year round, either here or in Portland where they have a second theater. They never are in just one play. They have parts in at least two or maybe three plays –sometimes a lead in one and a smaller part in another. It must be a scheduling nightmare for some organizer."

They watched as he strode up the busy street and stopped at the drug store as Stella Jacobs was coming out. Stella grabbed his arm as he tried to pass to go in the drug store and held him there for a discussion that looked very one-sided. After a minute, they could see him actually take her hand from his arm and turn his back to her. Sarah and Kitty moved closer to the spot in the street where Stella had stopped with an irritated but bemused expression on her face.

"Hello, Stella," Kitty said as they came closer to her. Stella, startled in her moment of put-down, glared fiercely at the women from Monterey, and with the briefest "Hello" moved quickly down the street.

"I'll bet he better watch out or she'll get it in for him. Maybe she lays a heavy hand with the actors as well as her son. Do you remember his name?"

"I forget but we could look it up in the program guide. Let's get on to the room. We could pick up some sandwiches and have our dinner on the green before the dancers arrive. There'll be plenty of room to spread out a blanket and enjoy a picnic."

"What a wonderful idea," Sarah said happily.

•••••••••

Charles McWorther hurried down the street, moving a little more swifty than normal. His handsome face was twisted with concern as he thought of the delay. He detested that woman and had wanted to get away as quickly as possible, but she kept talking and talking. He had left Elizabeth in a terrible state and had to get back immediately with her medicine. He hoped that his delay with Queen Stella would not upset his poor sick darling. He instinctively patted his pocket to make sure the prescription bottle was still there. He was at his wits end to help her. This was very strong medicine and he knew it must be addictive, but her pain was so bad when she didn't have it. This is the last refill for a while, he thought. Maybe she'll have to go to yet another doctor.

With that unhappy thought, he dashed up the steps of the two story apartment building, practically a stone's throw from the Elizabethan Theater, ran along the open passageway till he reached the last apartment. He flung open the door and moved softly to the bundle of clothing, legs and brown flowing hair that lay trembling in the middle of the bed.

"Elizabeth, darling. I'm home."

CHAPTER THREE

Kitty and Sarah were crushed in the crowd that tunneled into the two main doors of the outdoor theatre. The crowd thinned out in the open air lobby with rest rooms on one side and booths selling wine and food on the other.

"We need to rent cushions and blankets, Sarah," Kitty said as she led the way to the booth. "It gets really cold late at night. You'll be glad for a warm blanket."

They admired the stone wall that ringed the area. It was covered with shields for each year since the beginnings of Oregon Shakespeare Festival, listing the plays that had been shown that year, until the whole oeuvres was completed and the plays started again.

"It certainly gives you a sense of history." Sarah was impressed. Let's find our seats so we can read the story. I'm afraid that I've forgotten the plot of *The Winter's Tale.*"

"We're down near the front and in the center, because I sent the reservations in so early."

They adjusted their pillows and blankets, and Kitty stood to see if she recognized someone she knew in this huge crowd, but she couldn't see a familiar face in the large outdoor theater, even in the past when she and John were visiting every year, it was hard to see someone they knew.

Sarah was studing the synopsis. "Oh! Look! Charles McWorther is in this play. He's Florizel. Is that a big part?"

"No, that's a lot smaller role than Romeo. This system sure keeps the actors busy," Kitty replied.

Suddenly at the very top of the three-story stage a double window was thrown open and a trumpeter blew a few salutary notes and raised the flag for the Elizabethan stage. The show was about to begin.

•••••••••

The lights went on after the third act for the intermission. Both women sat enthralled in their seast for a minute before Kitty suggested that they go out and get a glass of wine or something to eat.

"That was so wonderful,the costumes. I really felt I was in old England," Sarah crooned.

"Lift thy body to the standing place, Sirrah" Kitty said as she led the way out the aisle.

There were lines at every booth. It was still warm, with a gentle breeze twisting the leaves on the trees that overhung the old Chattaqua stone wall that formed the perimeter of the Outdoor Theater. They stood in any line since there seemed to be no short one, and were surprised when a familiar grey-haired lady asked them what they wanted.

"Oh! You work here too, Mrs. Williams?" Kitty asked.

"I'm a volunteer with the Festival. Have been for years. Can I get you something?"

"Two glasses of white wine, please." Kitty and Sarah exchanged glances, expressing the feeling you get seeing someone you know in an unexpected place.

They sat on the stone wall at the perimeter sipping their wine until the bell sounded to return to their seats. Returning their glasses to the booth, Kitty saw Mrs. Williams with her back to the counter, putting something into a large black bag. Sarah pulled her arm as Kitty strained to see what was happening at the rear of the food cubicle.

"We better get back." Kitty reluctantly followed her friend in spite of her great curiosity.

•••••••••

The sun shown on the roses outside their room, and the freshly sprinkled grass sparkled with tiny water drops as Kitty and Sarah walked out the front door and down the steps. Kitty stopped and exclaimed, "Shouldn't we have the wonderful breakfast our mysterious Mrs. Williams serves in the dining room before we hit the town?"

"Oh, yes, I was so intent on getting to see the costumes, I almost forgot how hungry I am," Sarah replied.

"We could eat downtown, get some hot eggs and such, but the muffins are quite good here." Kitty's parsimonious spirit wouldn't let her pass up the free breakfast. She always considered it part of her "third generation Irish Potato Famine syndrome". Her mother always saved every scrap from dinner in the refrigerator. Eating leftovers was a familiar dinner procedure. Her mother was so frugal, she would save her basting thread, winding it on a special spool. Kitty was careful about money, but actually hated leftovers.

After some delicious fruit and cereal, the friends put a couple of muffins in their purses for a late morning snack.

"Thank you for another delicious breakfast. It was nice to see you last night," Kitty ventured. "Have you been with the Festival long?"

"I've devoted most of my life in Ashland to it. It's my joy and I'd protect it with my life." She disappeared through the kitchen door.

"Very worthy sentiments," Kitty shot to the departing back and held the door just as it was about to close. Walking into the kitchen, Kitty was not surprised to see the small black bag she had seen the night before. It appeared to be empty although there was a residue of crumbs on the bottom.

"Mrs. Williams, are you on the board of the Festival with Stella Jacobs?"

"Oh, no", she replied. "I'm just a small volunteer like a grain of sand on the big beach. Mrs. Jacobs is a very important person in town and has her fingers of a number of pies."

"What pies to you mean, Mrs. Williams?"

"Oh, I really couldn't say. I have to finish up here." She turned away from Kitty.

"It's been nice talking to you." She slipped back out the door to join Sarah.

"I guess we better get over to town," she told her, as Sarah nodded in fast agreement.

They reached the Welcome Center just as it opened and enjoyed the display of elaborate costumes that adorned the windows and every nook and cranny of the building.

"You'll enjoy the video of the history of the Festival. I don't mind seeing it again," Kitty said as they entered the small projection room.

"That was interesting," Sarah commented when they came out into the brightly lit room. "It does make it seem so much more important to know the history. No wonder you love to come up here."

"You know, they get over 100,000 people a year here but also give performances around the country. Now, do you want to take some pictures?"

They climbed the stairs to the costume room after taking a few shots of the cameo scenes in the rooms below. They were the only ones in the room and each selected the most dramatic capes or gowns on the rack. Choosing flamboyant hats to match each outfit they tried on, they snapped over a dozen pictures as queens, Calaban, Richard lll, or a simple jester. Before they knew it, it was a quarter to twelve.

"Look at the time," Kitty exclaimed. "We better put these away and get over to the bridge club if we want to play. I'm afraid we missed the talk on *Romeo and Juliet*. Maybe we can make the four o'clock show."

They ate their muffins as they crossed the green lawn between the theaters and walked down the back steps to the Lithia Park.

They entered the building just as everyone was settling down at the card tables.

"I'm glad you came," the director told them. "Now we'll have eight full tables. You can sit East/West with Joy and Marge."

They said, " Hello. How are you? It's good to see you again." almost in unison to their opponents who expressed pleasure at seeing the visitors again. John, the director, announced, "We now have eight full tables, since our visitors from Monterey, Kitty Malone and Sarah Peters have returned to play with us again. Let's welcome them."

Everyone called out "Welcome," and there was a general buzz of camaraderie until each person pulled out their hand from the stack of metal holders in the middle of the table. There was a concentrated silence as the players pulled out bidding cards from thebox to their right.

Kitty and Sarah were still a little keyed up from their morning's activities and, at the first table, defended moderately but not brilliantly. Marge and Joy were very good players and very pleasant. Both were in their mid sixties with neat grey hair and pants suits. Kitty and Sarah played one hand in a part score that made, but would probably have been better in three no-trump. "Sorry, partner," Sarah said. "I guess I should have bid no-trump since I have stoppers in most of the suits."

"It's a hard one to call. It would make two no-trump but it's hard to get there."

They moved on to the next table and greeted Stella and her son, Brian.

"Are you enjoying our beautiful city?" Stella seemed pleasant enough, after her rebuff on the street the day before.

"Yes, we love the park and the Welcome Center was wonderful," Sarah replied.

"I do quite a bit of work there when I get a chance," Stella returned. "Well, good luck!" as she pulled out her hand. Kitty was thrilled with her hand. She had twenty three high card points and calmly bid two clubs and Sarah bid four clubs showing ten or more points and good clubs. When Kitty bid 4 no-trump, asking for aces,

Sarah bid five hearts showing two. Kitty went to seven clubs because she didn't trust no-trump with her singleton ace of hearts.

Here is the hand:

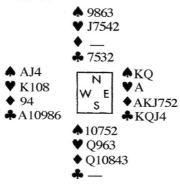

```
                    ♠ 9863
                    ♥ J7542
                    ♦ —
                    ♣ 7532
      ♠ AJ4          N        ♠ KQ
      ♥ K108      W     E      ♥ A
      ♦ 94           S         ♦ AKJ752
      ♣ A10986                 ♣ KQJ4
                    ♠ 10752
                    ♥ Q963
                    ♦ Q10843
                    ♣ —
```

South led the queen of hearts, taken by Kitty's ace. She checked trump by playing the king and noticed the bad break. She overtook her queen of spades with the ace and trumped a low heart in her hand. She drew trump, overtaking the jack with the ace and took the last trump with her ten. She played to the ace of diamonds and claimed since all of the other tricks were good. Others didn't pull trump before they started diamonds and went down one, so Kitty and Sarah got a high board. "Good playing, partner," said Sarah. The opponents chimed in as well.

After they finished the three boards and before they had to move to the next table, Kitty went to get more tea while. Brian Jacobs was also at the refreshment area.

"What are you majoring in at college, Brian?" Kitty was glad to get a space with him without the ever dominant Stella around.

"Communication, part of Social Studies," Brian answered.

"That's an interesting major. Do you learn to work with the media?"

"I don't know if I work with them. All the media in this country are pretty biased."

Kitty was pleased that he had a little independent thought.

"Well, it's a capitalist country so you're going to get a capitalist press." Kitty thought that was a pretty non-committal way to start a political discussion.

Brian perked right up. "Controlled by the corporations. Not much free enterprise in the press these days."

"The multi-national corporations do control it all. I work for a small newspaper in Monterey but they tow the conservative line. It's always hard to get any publicity for our United Nations Association events in our local paper."

"Yes, the multi-national corporations," Brian intoned, a spark of camaraderie passing between them with this use of a buzzword. The instant rapport between strangers who see they agree politically brought a warm feeling to Kitty.

"I was in the Model UN in high school here in Ashland but we don't have a club at the college. We have some good teachers but I guess there are none who want to go to the effort of starting a Model UN."

"Sometimes if the students get together and ask for it, a professor will come to the fore."

"I don't know about that, but we do have some active student groups. A bunch of us went to demonstrate in

Seattle against the World Trade Organization and their globalization policies"

"I went up with a group from Santa Cruz and Monterey Counties. It was very empowering for me. We actually closed down the meeting. What did you think of the demonstration?"

"It was a very exciting demonstration. But don't mention this to my Mom. She doesn't like me to get involved in political groups."

"I wouldn't think of saying anything. I was nice having this talk with you, Brian."

Kitty could see that the rest of the players were moving up to the next table. "I'm sure we'll have a chance to talk again while we're in Ashland."

She joined the players at the last table for the day, and again she and Sarah held their own with good defense against two of the contracts so that they got a next to the top and top score on each of those boards. The game Sarah played in three no-trump was almost flat, everybody except one pair bidding and making the same score.

They felt pretty good as they finished that game and stood at the door to see the results of the scores printed out by the computer. It was always fun to see how they did in relation to other players. Since they were rated in Flight B, by the number of points they had accumulated, Kitty was pleased to see that they came in second in the club in B. The A players, with many more master points, had made a better percentage, but she felt they had done well that day. They were standing around in an air of affability when Kitty saw Brian Jacobs rush to the front door, after giving his mother a short pat on the head.

"I'll see you in a few hours. Got lots of errands."

Stella looked very upset and seemed as if she held back the urge to grab her son's jacket as he dashed by.

"These young people. Always in a rush," she observed to no one in particular.

"He's a fine looking boy. He must have lots of girlfriends." Kitty said to Stella as they stood watching him disappear across the street and into the park.

"Not really," Stella replied moodily. "He's got many interests and not much time for that sort of thing."

She was concerned because Brian had seemed very remote the last few days, with his head in the clouds. She had to speak a few times to him to get his attention.

Stella had been a romantic herself when she was his age growing up in Brentwood and dreaming of a career as an actress. She'd learned to act all right, after she fell deeply in love with Oscar Jacobs, never in any play or movie but in real life, keeping her love a secret from her demanding parents until a bulging belly had forced the issue. She had learned to help his career, pushing him forward, using her parents' connections with producers and wealthy backers. She had learned to be tough, to get what she wanted for her small family. Her boy's and Oscar's welfare was all she cared about so she had to be very strict with Brian, keep him from mistakes and bad companions, since Oscar seldom came to Ashland, now, because of his film work in Hollywood. She wondered why Brian was so moony the last few days. I'll have to put more limits on his time away from me, she thought.

•••••••••

Juanita sat on a creekside bench in one of the far sections of the long narrow park that seemed more of an adornment to Ashland Creek than a park in the fullest sense, not that she didn't love every part of it. The dirt path was bordered by perennial, low growing shrubs. The rhododendrons were fully in bloom, dark purple blossoms bordered by pink mountain laurel edging some of the paths. She had spent many hours exploring the twists and turns of the park on the creekside and also across the road that followed up the sloping hill. She loved the little Japanese Garden and the fountain area. But the creekside with tables and benches in hidden coves was her favorite. This is where she had asked Brian to meet her. She felt a tingle just thinking about him. She had never felt this way before, a sort of warm flush whenever she thought of him. She had told B.J. that she was coming to the top level near the small maintenance house, in case Brian got lost and couldn't find her.

She lay back on a bench. Everywhere she looked there were so many different types of trees–maple, oak and ash filled the skyline. Always the creek rushed, one short waterfall eddying into pools before spilling over smooth rocks to the next level rushing headlong for miles. The two ponds in the park with dozens of ducks were not fed by the creek and were a thick green with a high nitrogen content.

Her reverie was startled by a noise on the path. There he was coming up the path toward her. She stood and waited until he was very close and without a word put her arms around him and pushed her lean young body against his strong chest. His mouth found hers and their tongues met with a smooth blend of their breath.

"Oh, my darling. I haven't stopped thinking of you since yesterday. I could hardly sleep dreaming of your beautiful lips, your eyes like violets in a sunny field. I know there could never be another for me. You are my dream, my darling Juanita."

He kissed her again and held her tightly.

"I've never felt like this before. You read about love and you see lovers in the movies, but you can't imagine how it feels when it happens to you," she told him.

"Then you do love me, just as I love you. I've had some girlfriends in college but this feeling is something I've never had before. It's a wonderful feeling. I want to be with you every minute and with no one else." Brian took her hand gently in his as he walked toward the small maintenance house.

"Do you know if that is open?" he asked gently.

"I don't know. We could see." And they walked hand in hand toward the small stone house set back from the landscaped paths of the park.

Brian turned the knob but it was locked. "Let's see if this is as formidable as it looks." He took out a small pen knife and inserted the blade in the lock and gave a quick turn as he moved the knob.

"Voila! Just like a safe-cracker."

Juanita gave an admiring laugh and stepped into the doorway.

"No, let me carry you, my bride." Brian swept her into his arms and walked into the tiny cement floored cabin.

"It's very cozy but quite dark." Juanita's eyes were focusing in the dim room that had only a tiny upper window.

Brian picked up a couple of empty burlap bags, laying them on the floor, he draped his jacket over them.

"All the comforts of home," he said, breathlessly as he knelt, taking her hand to pull her next to him.

"We can pretend that this is our home and that we are married and live all alone in the world."

"That would be so wonderful," she replied openly though she had a little sense of nervousness since she knew what to expect but had never actually done it before.

They kissed for a long time and he kissed her breasts and breathed into her ears.

"I do want to be your bride, but I've never done this before," she told him.

"I know. I will be so gentle, you'll never feel a thing."

"Well, I hope I feel something!" They both laughed as he carefully took off her clothes and then his own. They could just barely see each other in the pale light but to them their bodies together were the most beautiful in the world. They never noticed the grey-brown figure that peered in the half shuttered window on the stone house.

•••••••••

The grey-brown hassock hung loosely from the hook on the wall and the sturdy figure in green overalls that had just flung it there sniffed the air like a greyhound. There was a cloying odor of sex about the room. A quick look assured that all the cabinets were closed. The stark single bulb from the ceiling shone on two standard metal cabinets against the far wall and just below the half blocked window another cabinet thrusting on wooden legs –jutted out into the room. The metal cabinets contained different types of chemicals for use in Lithia Park. The one on the right held organic fertilizers, bags of potassium,

Potash, Vitamin B1, Dial soaps to keep the deer off young plants, snail bait made of pepper and beer, etc. The left cabinet contained enough poison to kill all the bugs in Oregon.

When the wooden doors of the center cabinet were opened, a mini laboratory was laid out with a Bunsen burner, glass flasks, petri dishes and all the equipment of a mad scientist.

This was B.J.'s sole domain, with an official title of "Upper Park Attendant". The real work was more of a hydroponic gardener/sewage eradicator. "Too many ducks!" was B.J.'s refrain as the problem of the unhealthy green of the upper and especially lower pond deepened. Only severe measures could solve the situation. The nitrogen feeding plants B.J. had placed in a ring in the center of the upper pond was taking forever to make the slightest pH change in the water and the consistency was still a pea soup viscosity. The pond water was kept distinctly away from the precious Lithia water of the creek. The acrid, metallic water, so treasured for it's medical cures in the special fountain set up in the plaza, would not be conducive to duck breeding. Mixing the two would only ruin both. The pond waters were pumped through a series of old pipes with gentle rock waterfalls through the two large pond systems. Nothing, not even the aeration of the falls, helped the duck effluence. Stern measures were needed and B.J. worked silently at the little laboratory table.

.

●●●●●●●●●●

Kitty turned over in her narrow twin bed to look at her travel clock. It was already 9 o'clock. She looked at Sarah still asleep under the covers. I'll just let her sleep since we don't have any plays today or any bridge, she thought. She turned over and tried

to remember what she was dreaming. She knew there was a murder in it. Sort of fuzzy, like a veil was hanging over her thoughts, but she could remember enough to know that she'd had a terrible premonition of disaster. Someone had been killed and she could see a murderer sneaking out of the room. She looked hard but couldn't tell who it was or who was killed. She had always been an avid reader of mysteries and had developed a perceptive sense of the facts of a case. She had been instrumental in solving a mystery right in her own back yard last year and now considered herself an armchair detective. She didn't like the feeling she was getting at the bridge club. As she turned in her early morning bed, the dream, a premonition of trouble to come, was heavy in her heart and mind.

"What are you sighing about, Kitty?" Sarah turned over to face her friend.

"I just had a bad dream. There was a murder and it seemed to be right here in Ashland."

"Oh, dear. I hope you're not right. It's just a bad dream. What shall we do today?"

"We can drive to Jacksonville. It's a wonderful little town with a great children's museum and living history on the main streets."

"By living history, do you mean actors take parts and pretend they are living in a different time? I saw that once in Plymouth. There were great actors on the replica of the Mayflower."

"Well, I don't think they're actors. Just folks from the town with old fashioned costumes. The period isn't so long ago you know, maybe a hundred years or so."

"That sounds like a great trip. Is it far?"

"No, it's just the next town. Maybe half an hour by car. If you want to go, we could have our breakfast here and take a leisurely drive to Jackson. Does that sound good?"

"That sounds great!"

After a full breakfast, they walked past the kitchen door where the car was parked. Kitty noticed a note pad that had fallen from the garbage and kicked it with her foot. She could see that it was almost new, so she picked it up as they got into the Camry and turned North on Main Street. They followed Route 99 instead of getting on the parallel US 5 so that they could see the farms and small town of Talent.

"John always bought his hats from the small farmhouse turned hat factory in Talent. The Hat People. He loved their style when he first noticed them at one of the Saturday craft fairs at Ashland."

Kitty was silent for a few miles as she remembered her days of vacationing with John. It was nice to have company so she was not missing him quite as much as she'd expected to when she came to this area.

They turned off the main highway at Phoenix and passed the verdant farms and orchards until they suddenlyarrived at the outskirts of the heritage town of Jacksonville. Parking on the Main Street, they strolled past the restored buildings . Most were closed but they could look in the windows of a hundred year old bar with a sign "United States Hotel Building". An ancient bank seemed open for business as it had been more than a century before. Unique gift shops and book stores were nestled between the larger antique buildings. There was a pleasant bustle to the streets and the women picked up some brochures about the town. They saw the location of one of the living history houses just a few blocks up the main drag.

They stopped in a charming restaurant and had salmon filets and green salads. When she opened her purse to pay her share of the bill, Kitty saw the note book she'd thrown in there. Too nice to throw away, she had thought, and now she examined it more carefully. The front was empty but further back were figures and words that didn't make sense. Thinking that she could still use the front half, she pushed it back in her purse wondering briefly if the notebook belonged to someone at their bed and breakfast.

They walked the two blocks to the one-story clapboard house. A girl in a full length cotton dress greeted them at the door and they saw a sitting room where two women were sewing on a patch work quilt. Intricate patterns of pink cotton and flowered squares were being sewn by hand. The seamstresses explained that they make the patches by hand and put the batting and backing on by machine, pointing to an old Singer in the corner. A few quilts were stacked on the table by the window with price tags discreetly tucked under the corner. Kitty and Sarah thought they were quite reasonable considering all the hand work. In the kitchen a man in jeans was bringing in wood for a large, black iron stove that had various sized rings in the top. It looked like bread was being made on the center kitchen table which held a few covered ceramic bowls. One loaf was on a breadboard being kneaded by a aproned matronly woman.

"That was really charming. *All the world's a stage and all the men and women merely players,*" Sarah said as they left after watching the household chores unfold for almost an hour.

" Ah! *They have their exits and their entrances; and one man in his time plays many parts.* You're very good, Sarah. Would you like to see the Children's Museum before we go back?"

"Sure!" Sarah was enjoying this trip back into history. The brick building housing the unique museum was only two blocks away. Toys from hundreds of years ago were attractively set in small alcoves in the lower floor. The second floor was devoted to a tribute to Peewee the Clown.

On the way back to Ashland, they stopped at the Jackson and Perkins rose garden that stretched for blocks in front of a brick factory building. Each square was color keyed to a separate species and all were in full glorious bloom.

"What a wonderful display of roses!" Sarah exclaimed. "I'm so glad I came with you. You are a great guide and I love everything I've seen so far." Little did they know that as they enjoyed the roses, a great tragedy was unfolding back in Ashland.

●●●●●●●●●●

On Thursday afternoon after a day of shopping, a day without bridge, Stella drove the green Lexus up the steep hills north of town, annoyed that Brian hadn't informed her until the last minute that he wasn't going to drive her home. She pulled into the drive in front of a large Victorian house set far back from the street, clicked the garage opener and inched her car into the narrow space. Too bad they hadn't made bigger garages when they remodeled the old house. Taking a substantially well-built house, the remodel had created a glorious living, dining and wrap-around porch that overlooked the valley where Ashland nestled.

The kitchen and two baths had been fitted with the latest appliances and fixtures, but the garage had seemed too much a part of the decor to change it much. Brian had no trouble swinging into it, giving her a warm feeling thinking of his agility, but she was always afraid she was going to hit one of the walls. Not even room to store junk in it, she thought, as she went up the three stairs into the family room. She poured a glass of soda from a bottle she found and, kicking off her shoes, stretched out on the sofa and clicked on the TV.

That was where Brian found her that evening when he came home, still in a haze of love.

" Mom, sorry to be so late. I met a few friends and we got talking." He stopped as he looked carefully at her lifeless body.

"Mom! What is it? Are you asleep?" He touched her and jumped back from the cold feeling of her skin.

He went to the phone and called their doctor. "My mother is lying in the living room. I think she's dead, she feels so cold." Then he called his father in Los Angeles.

He explained that he'd called the doctor and was waiting for him now and promised to call as soon as the doctor arrived.

Brian sat catatonically on the couch until Dr. Brand rang the bell, and was white faced as he opened the door to admit the doctor. After examining the body carefully, Dr. Brand gently said, "I'm afraid she dead, Brian. There are no signs of life."

"What did she die from?"

"I'd have to do an autopsy, but it could be something in this glass on the rug beside her. We better call the police."

"Oh my God. You mean she was poisoned? I have to call my father back. "

Brian took the phone and dialed his father's number in Los Angeles.

He turned the phone over to Dr. Brand who talked briefly to Oscar. He turned to the stricken boy.

"Your father's leaving on the next plane. He'll call the police, he says, but doesn't want to do anything until he gets here to take charge." Brian's face was ashen, the blood drained out of his cheeks, and he was having a hard time breathing. Dr. Brand checked Brian's pulse and looked in his eyes.

"I'm going to give you something to calm your nerves," he said as he opened his bag for a bottle of pills.

"I don't think I need anything. I'm just shocked." His hands were trembling. "Well, maybe I should take an aspirin to calm me till Dad comes."

The Doctor got a glass of water from the kitchen and gave him two pills. "These are a little stronger than Aspirin but will relax you. Now try to rest until Oscar comes home."

CHAPTER FOUR

Oscar Jacobs threw a few articles into an overnight bag and, taking well-known short cuts, maneuvered through traffic to LAX. His flight, first to Portland and then the shuttle to Medford, would bring him to Brian in about four hours if his connections worked out. He felt that things always worked out for him so he didn't worry too much about the connections. He was concerned that his romantic, beautiful son wouldn't be able to handle something like this.

Oscar was a self-made man, scratching his way up from a poor neighborhood in Los Angeles. Son of a greengrocer and a seamstress, he had not had a comfortable childhood. Too many children, not enough work for the family to support all the three boys and four girls. None of his siblings had made anything of themselves, and he hardly saw them anymore.

He was well-groomed, expensively tanned and fit after many years with a personal trainer, but he was almost completely bald. He'd often thought about implanted hair or a hairpiece, but everyone knew him as bald and it was more embarrassing to suddenly have hair. He was thankful that there were stars like Yul Brenner and Kojak, so it had stopped bothering him long ago. Stella didn't seem to mind. Anyway they'd gone their own ways long ago.

He pulled into the long-term parking. No telling how long this would take and there's no point in paying the daily fees, he thought. It was after he got off the airline bus and was waiting in line with his ticket already confirmed that it suddenly dawned on him that he wouldn't be seeing Stella– that Stella was dead.

•••••••••

Kitty and Sarah walked the short blocks to Janet's Shakespearean Museum when they came back from their trip to Jacksonville. It was close to four o'clock when they reached the front door and were dismayed to see a note pinned there. "Closed until 11 am Friday" was inscribed in a delicate hand.

"That's a shame," said Kitty in a disappointed tone, "But we can come back in the morning." They walked back to the Town Square. They had decided that the delicatessen facing Ashland Creek was a good place to have dinner before the Green Show. As they passed the square going toward the park, a tall thin figure was coming down the road. Kitty pointed and said to Sarah, "Isn't that the monk-like figure we saw on our first night in town?"

"Yes, I see. Is that a man or a woman? Hard to tell, but he's coming really fast, almost running."

B.J. stopped the headlong rush down hill as the Town Square came into view. Pulling out a soft cigarette pack and pausing to light up, B.J. calmly walked to a bench and sat down, breathing heavily but slower now.

'That is an unusual looking person," Kitty said as they crossed over to the deli, being careful not to stare at the dejected figure sprawled on the bench.

"Oh look! There's that wonderful actor, Charles McWorther."

As they watched, they saw a strange scene unfold. The actor walked up to the monk-like figure and leaned over to speak, close to the hood. The homespun hood gave a negative shake and the actor went to a man on the next bench and asked him something. The actor held out his hand and, to the two women watching, it looked like something was exchanged between them.

Charles McWorther pushed his hand quickly into his pocket and with his distinctive swagger, turned on his heels. The man who had given him something rose and followed a little behind but quickened his pace to cross the street so they were both going up the Bowmer steps together.

The second man showed the actor something that stopped him in his tracks. There seemed to be a heated but hushed argument and the second man placed a firm arm on the actor's shoulder and steered him toward a car parked on the street. They got in and car pulled out as the girls continued to stare.

"What was that?" Sarah asked Kitty with her eyes wide and startled.

"I think we just witnessed a sting, just like they show on television. I can't imagine what that beautiful actor would be doing buying drugs. "

"Wow! This certainly is an interesting city!" Sarah panted. Entering the restaurant, neither of them found they had much of an appetite.

•••••••••

On Friday morning they showed up at Janet's. They

were pleased to see the hunter green and white banner hung out on the pole in the yard. They were the first ones there and looked more carefully around the enlarged living room. Janet greeted them pleasantly but was busy sorting cards and disappeared behind her carved wooden screen for quite a few minutes. Another couple arrived, a middle aged man and wife and Kitty explained that Janet was in her kitchen and would be out in a minute. When a third group arrived, a family with a teenaged boy, Janet finally came out to greet them. She explained the cost of the lecture, which was to start in a few minutes, and collected the modest fee into her drawer at the front desk.

The girls enjoyed the lecture on *Romeo and Juliet* that Janet delivered. With seven paying customers filling her comfortable chairs, Janet expanded on her theory that Friar Lawrence was Juliet's mother's former lover. It had seemed a little farfetched to Kitty and Sarah so they good naturedly took it with a grain of salt. There was an awed silence as she developed her proof that Father Lawrence had deliberately caused the tragic deaths. The others hadn't seen the play yet so were tongue-tied, but Kitty questioned Janet about where in the text she had developed this theory.

Janet was emphatic that with Shakespeare you had to look for motives behind the lines. Shakespeare, she said, had a reason for everything he wrote, so there had to be some logical reason behind everything he put in his plays. Kitty thought he was allowed more artistic license than Janet gave him but she changed the subject.

"We missed you for the tea lecture yesterday," Kitty told her. A faint blush colored Janet's open face.

"I'm sorry. I had errands in the afternoon. There's never enough time to do everything."

"Of course, but we came back as you see. Do you run this museum all by yourself?"

"Yes. It's a lot of work, but I love it," she replied, her blush fading as she showed her cards to the other customers.

"We enjoyed the lecture. We'll come again, maybe to The Winter's Tale lecture, since we've seen that performance."

"Yes, do come again," Janet called after them.

•••••••••

They arrived early for the afternoon session at the bridge club. The tables began to fill up, when the phone rang and the director, looking very startled, called for everyone's attention.

"I've just received word of a terrible tragedy. It seems hard to believe, but it seems that Stella Jacobs died yesterday afternoon." There was a strong gasp throughout the entire room.

"What happened?" a number of people asked.

"I don't know the details, but her husband has arrived and asked that she be laid out in her home. Anyone who wishes to pay their respects can visit."

Another murmur covered the room.

"Isn't that unusual?" Kitty asked the other pair at her table. "I thought she was Jewish and so should be buried right away."

Page 57

"Obviously not. Maybe Oscar felt that this is what she would have wanted," Marge told the group at the table. "I think we should go pay our respects after the game," she said to her partner. "She was not a good friend, but I enjoyed playing bridge with her. I feel that it's a big loss to Ashland"

The game was as quiet as ever, but between shifts to different tables, there were no raised voices or laughter. It was a very somber afternoon.

When Sarah and Kitty were playing with two regulars later in the afternoon, they had one interesting hand. South opened one club and Sarah doubled. North passed and Kitty, East, bid two hearts. Passed to Sarah who bid two spades. Kitty bid three spades and Sarah went to game in spades. Passed out.

The lead was the ace of clubs, with a negative two signal from South. Sarah took the diamond switch, cashed another diamond, and trumped a third diamond. Next she led low from the trumps, taking the trick with her jack. The ace of trumps brought down the king. All the rest of the cards held making five, a good board.

This was the deal.

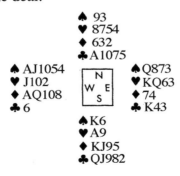

```
                    ♠ 93
                    ♥ 8754
                    ♦ 632
                    ♣ A1075
    ♠ AJ1054        ┌──────┐      ♠ Q873
    ♥ J102          │   N  │      ♥ KQ63
    ♦ AQ108         │ W  E │      ♦ 74
    ♣ 6             │   S  │      ♣ K43
                    └──────┘
                    ♠ K6
                    ♥ A9
                    ♦ KJ95
                    ♣ QJ982
```

At 3:30 groups huddled indecisively at the door. Kitty asked Marge if she and her partner were going to drive up to Stella's house.

"Yes, we're going there now," she answered in a slightly surprised tone of voice. "Did you, do you want to go?"

"If it would be convenient for you, Marge. We don't want to intrude but we thought that Stella Jacobs was a very interesting woman."

"Yes, she was that, very interesting. Well, you can come with us if you want. We're just going up for a brief stay."

The four of them got into Marge's white Toyota and slowly drove up the hill behind Ashland Creek to a beautiful Victorian house isolated on a small knoll.

"What a marvelous location," Sarah was awed by the view. "You can see the whole valley."

"Stella loved this house. Never wanted to move back to L.A. after she and Oscar moved here. He wasn't here that often. I think they went their seperate ways."

They walked up the wide steps onto the porch and rang the bell at the ornate front door with stained glass panels. A maid ushered them into the entry. They handed her the large floral bouquet they'd chipped in on at the Ashland Florist before they drove up. The maid told them that Oscar was in the living room, a room that stretched toward the back of the house. The study was to the left and a dining room, with a full buffet set out on the table, was on the right.

"We're friends of Stella's from the bridge club, Oscar. I'm Marge Chapin. We're so shocked and so sorry for you." And she introduced the others.

"Yes, I remember you, Marge. Thank you for coming.

I arrived yesterday evening and you know she looked so beautiful, I just wanted to be with her for awhile. I know that this is unusual but she just doesn't seem dead to me." His voice broke and he turned away. Turning back, he said, "Stella is here in the rear of the living room."

They followed him and noticed Brian, dry-eyed and bewildered on a straight back chair off to the side. Stella's body was draped in white and on a platform near the back wall. Flowers lined the sides of the room. The indirect lighting softened her features. She did look very peaceful and beautiful.

Kitty sat near Brian, as Marge and Joy talked softly to his father.

"This happened yesterday, after bridge?" Kitty questioned gently. "Do you know what happened?"

Brian started briefly and stammered. "I don't know. When I came back to the house around six or seven, I found her on the sofa. I called the doctor and my Dad. He wanted everything to stay the way it was. He came in late last night and, and made all the arrangements."

"What did the doctor say was the cause of death?"

"He didn't know. There was a glass on the floor. I don't know what happened."

"Did you call the police? Doesn't the doctor have to call the police."

"No, Dad wanted to handle everything. Dr. Bland has been in Ashland forever and has been our family doctor since we moved here. I guess he wanted to leave it up to Dad." He got up to go to the front door as the bell rang. Oscar was starting to move away from the group of women.

"I'll go, Dad." He seemed anxious to get away from questions.

When he opened the door, Juanita and Wanda were on the porch. Juanita tearfully put her arms around Brian, and Wanda put her hand gently on his shoulder. His back shook with silent sobs.

"I'm all right, " he told them. "It's just so hard to believe. She's here you know and looks so peaceful."

He took Juanita's hand and facing Wanda, told her, "I'm very much in love with your daughter. I want her to be my wife. Someday," he added after a pause realizing his lover's tender young age.

"There's time to talk of that when you're out of college. You are both so young." Wanda didn't want to lay a heavy trip on the couple after her years of giving so much freedom to her beautiful daughter.

"I'll give my condolences to your father," Wanda said as she slipped past him and out into the living room.

The two lovers just stood holding hands. Juanita had never known death in her young life and felt embarrassed to mention it, to put her feelings into words to soothe him, so all she could do was put her arms around him again and bury her face in his shoulder. He took her hand and leading her into the dining area, said softly,

"Don't feel bad. I'm OK. It's my father I'm worried about. He's taken it very badly. I found him sitting beside her with a razor. I was afraid he was going to kill himself."

"How terrible. Is he better now?"

"Yes, he seems calmer now more accepting."

"How did she die? Did someone kill her?" Juanita asked.

"The doctor said she may have been poisoned. He wasn't sure but my father told him over the phone to leave everything until he got here to sort it out."

"The doctor's allowed to do that? Not call the police if something is suspicious?"

Juanita's clear thinking, a naivete about worldly pressures cut through the cloud of family position and power in this small town.

"I guess that has to be done. I'll leave it up to Dad. To think that this must have happened while we were together in the park."

"When did she die?"

"It must have been just before I got home at 7 o'clock. That's when I felt for her pulse."

"Did she do it to herself?"

"That may be what they will decide, but she didn't leave a note or anything. Do you want a glass of wine?" he asked as he poured a glass for himself.

"I don't drink. Thank you, Brian," she said sweetly.

So engrossed were they in their feelings for each other that they didn't even see Kitty standing by the table with a small plate and glass of wine. Kitty, for her part, was too diffident to make her presence known but couldn't help but overhear everything the young couple said, even though it was in a hushed tone. She turned and left the room, moving up to Sarah who was looking out of the bay window to the expanse of the valley below.

"This may have been a murder," she said in a whisper. "I overheard Brian say that the doctor thought that Stella had been poisoned."

"Really," Sarah's eyes opened wide. "Are the police...?"

"They weren't called," Kitty broke in. "Mr. Jacobs forbade it until his arrival. I always seem to stumble into these things," she said, almost to herself. She had worked with the Monterey police in solving two murders last year.

Sarah stared at her. "You mean this is really another murder?"

"Maybe I should speak to Mr. Jacobs," Kitty interjected. "It's not right that he doesn't call the police and why would he want to keep her here in the house? It's not natural." Sarah nodded silently.

Kitty walked to Oscar Jacobs as he stood by the side of his wife's casket. His shoulders were bent as if holding a heavy burden, his eyes fixed on Stella's face. Kitty stood by his side for a full minute before he, feeling her presence penetrate his self enclosed world, turned to speak to her.

"Yes, you are a friend of Stella's?"

"I'm Kitty Malone. Not a long time friend of your wife, just played bridge with her the last few days, and she didn't seem depressed or suicidal to me. How do you explain her death?"

"It would be hard to imagine Stella taking her own life. She may have had enemies. She was a strong, powerful woman. I should find out the reasons," he broke off.

"Shouldn't you call the police to investigate?"

"But they would autopsy the body, cut her up. I can't stand the thought."

"But you can't keep her here long."

"Yes, I know. I'll call the in ... in the morning." He

turned away and went to his son who was still talking quietly to Juanita.

Kitty looked closely at the corpse. She touched the skin of her arm, which seemed soft, not hard like most cadavers. How unusual, she thought. So cold but still so soft.

Oscar in the meantime had taken his son's arm and looked questioningly at the beautiful young girl standing in front of them.

"Dad, this is Juanita West, my girlfriend," he said simply.

"I'm glad to meet you." His approval was favorable, implicit in his warm tone. He appraised her carefully from her soft blond hair falling over her shoulders, her astute blue eyes, firm chin, slender figure in a well fitting summer dress to her sensible sandals.

"She's beautiful, Brian. I congratulate you on your choice."

"This is my mother, Wanda West," Juanita said smiling at his approval.

As Oscar turned, his breath came quickly and scenes of a evening on the beach of Malibu filled his mind.

"I'm glad to see you. It seems we've met before a number of years ago."

"Yes, Oscar, that's right," Wanda said softly.

●●●●●●●●●

Ardemis Grey looked startled.

"Charles McWhorther, what are you doing here?" The detective looked down at the sheet in front of him with disbelief. "Is this some mistake, Ralph?" He asked the arresting officer, a man dressed in jeans, not a uniform. "This is Charles McWhorter, one of the main stars of the Shakespeare Theater." Turning to Charles, he smiled. "I enjoyed you very much in *Romeo & Juliet*. Now what's this all about?"

"I was trying to buy some medicine for my wife. She's in a lot of pain and these drugs seem to be the only thing to help her."

Charles spoke softly and with deep feeling. He was so torn by emotion that he could hardly talk at all.

"Your wife should go to a doctor, or be in a hospital, not be needing drugs you have to buy on the street. What's wrong with her?"

"She's had anxiety attacks, then sprained her leg. She started using pain killing drugs and now she needs them all the time. We do have a doctor but he won't renew the prescription. I didn't know where to turn."

Inspector Grey was quiet for a minute, then he turned to the plainclothes man.

"Ralph, I'm going to take responsibility for this myself. I'll book him but let him out on OR so he can continue work. We'll set the hearing for next Monday. He should be free then–no theater."

He filled out the forms as Ralph left the precinct.

"There's nothing you can do for your wife until you get her in a hospital. Can you get your doctor and arrange that?"

"I don't know if he will do that. He's only seen her a few times and he's very busy."

"This is important enough to call him right now. What's

his name? I can't let you go without making some arrangements for your wife."

Charles gave him the name with great relief. This is the way the police should be, he thought, still not quite believing it was real.

Inspector Grey explained the importance to the doctor's exchange and soon had him on the line.

He explained the situation and asked if the doctor would arrange some immediate treatment for Mrs. McWhorter. "It must be quite desperate for him to go out on the street like that, especially here in Ashland." He paused while he listened to the doctor, then turned to Charles.

"He's going to arrange a hospital room in Medford. He'll call ahead and you can bring her there. Please sign these papers and be here on Monday for the hearing. You do have to go before a Judge. I'm sure under the circumstances it will just be probation."

"I can't thank you enough, Inspector Grey. This is such a relief. I was at my wit's end."

"Well, I'm a fan of yours and we appreciate all that the Theater has done for Ashland. Let me know how everything turns out."

"Yes, Of course and thanks again." Charles swung out the door and raced down the quiet streets to his apartment to drive his poor wife to Medford.

•••••••••

Kitty and Sarah were very quiet as they drove down the hill with Marge and Joy, who dropped them at the street in front of the Hathaway Arms.

"What's the matter, Kitty? You're so solemn. What are you thinking?"

"This is a very strange situation, Sarah. It's probably murder and I'm sure she had enough enemies. But the whole scene up at the house was so strange and yet so familiar in some ..." Her words trailed off and she was very quiet as she walked up the concrete drive and into their house.

"I'll just have to think about it."

●●●●●●●●●●

From her years at bridge, and dozens of mysteries that she had read, Kitty had developed a strong sense of intuition. This helped her at the bridge table, what is called table sense, and she could tell, most of the time, if a finesse was going to work. She had worked with Mark Lipsky, a detective in Monterey, in solving a double murder last year. Although she had made a few wrong turns early in that investigation, she was able to put the facts together and trap the murderer.

There were certainly some suspicious characters lurking around this case, she thought. Although she hadn't heard anyone speak against her at the club, no one seemed to like Stella Jacobs, except her son and husband. At least it seemed that they did. Janet certainly was an enemy, or had been made so by Stella. Kitty let her thoughts ramble on as she lay back on her comfy bed to catch a little rest before the next play.

What about Juanita and Wanda? They seemed so perfectly sweet, almost too much so. And then there was that actor who seemed to hate her when she'd seen them on the street, and he certainly must be involved in drugs. There could be other characters as well. So far she had nothing to go to the police with. Where were the police, she suddenly wondered? There couldn't have been an autopsy or the body of Stella Jacobs would not still be lying in the living room on Summit Street. She couldn't imagine that she was the only one who thought it was murder. Well, she wasn't going to let it ruin her vacation. All she wanted to do was see plays and play bridge. So she would try not to think about it.

"I'm glad we have tickets for the Black Swan tonight," she told Sarah. "I just want to really forget about this mess. Oh, I forgot, we have tickets for The Feast of Will tonight before the play."

"What a busy schedule we have," complained Sarah. "What is the Feast of Will?"

"It's wonderful! The Oregon Shakespeare Festival Committee puts on a dinner for the whole community in Lithia Park on the first Friday at the opening of the outdoor theatre. It's quite good–fried chicken, salad, punch and desert, a delicious pecan tart they make especially for this event. There's very good entertainment, bagpipes and the Green Musicians, sometimes a choral group as well. You'll love it."

"OK. But tomorrow we've got to rest."

"Absolutely," Kitty assured her.

●●●●●●●●●●

More than two hundred people lined the paths as they waited for the Feast of Will to pull back the ribbons that blocked the festive section of the park that had dozens of flower laden tables lined up. The line moved quickly as people moved to four separate serving lines. Kitty and Sarah filled their plates and walked to the tables. They didn't see anyone they knew so they took some empty seats and greeted the young couple who were seated opposite them.

"This certainly went quickly once they started serving." Kitty observed. "Is this your first time here?" she smiled at the couple. They looked too young to have been coming here before.

"Oh no," they spoke together. Then the young man explained. "We've been coming here for years. They've streamlined the serving line for the Feast. I can remember when we had to wait for hours in the line, when there was only one serving station."

"Yes, I can remember that. After one experience, I bought a dinner and ate it on the lawn as I watched the hungry Feastgoers. It was fun to watch the bagpipers line up and practice before they paraded into the party."

"Well, that was clever of you. But most people just wanted to support the Festival. It is a major fundraiser you know, so they waited their turn. I think it is much better now though." Kitty blushed a little at the gentle put-down. She let it slide as the entertainment was about to begin. They enjoyed the bagpipers and the Irish dancers, with their green dresses and flailing feet. There was a small local choral group, dressed in long white gowns, flowered halos on their heads, accompanied by the Festival Green Players. It was a very good show. The audience rose and followed the musical group as they moved through the Park up to the stage of the Green Players.

Kitty and Sarah decided not to watch the show since they had seen it on Tuesday.

"Let's go to the coffee house where Wanda has her mural," Kitty suggested, and they walked over to the store close to the Black Swan.

The large bucolic mural filled the south wall.

"It's really beautiful, very reminiscent of the Oregon countryside though stylized. I love the colors," Kitty said.

"Look at that booth in the back, Kitty. Isn't that Wanda with Oscar Jacobs?"

"You're right. Somehow I don't think we should go over and interrupt. They look pretty cozy. Anyway we better go over to the Black Swan so we don't miss the play. They won't let us in late you know."

They walked out without ordering coffee, Kitty wondering why the two parents of the young lovers were together. Were they solicitous about their kids or was there something else.

●●●●●●●●●●

Oscar had been really surprised to see Wanda. It had been a long time ago, but the memory was there. It amazed him that just the slightest variation of the features, the nose, eyes, shape of the face could so distinguish one person from another that even after, what was it, ten or twelve years, the memory was clear as a bell. He used to work out on the beach, not muscle beach, but a quieter spot closer to Malibu where he and some friends could play volleyball and do some gymnastics.

He had noticed her when she had a booth set up for small artist fair that ran along the street facing the ocean. He saw that she was beautiful, a wholesome look with an ethereal air from the shake of her head to her delicate hand movements. But he was only interested in the art work. He was working for a small independent film company and he had to wear many hats–director, casting director, as well as art director. A total director, one might say. The story was about a woman artist who was going mad. Her husband was cheating and her teenage kids were potheads. Not a happy story although they thought up a happy ending for popular consumption. He wasn't pleased with the artwork in the film. It had to be original because he couldn't use Matisse, so he had been going along the booths at the ocean fair looking briefly at the pedestrian art.

Her beauty attracted him first, but her art work and colors were vibrant, her form unique. There seemed to be a perception under the facile impressionistic presentation. She was a more serious artist than the others at the fair. He looked through her watercolors that were piled on the table. There were a few oils on the easels set up in front of her chair, but he was drawn to the light but vivid colors of her smaller work.

She was busy talking to someone. There was a small child at her feet who seemed to be hers. He waited patiently for her to finish her conversation with a man who had bought a painting and was trying to get her to deliver it. It seemed like he was hitting on her but she handled it in a very businesslike way. She was polite but she didn't deliver. Oscar thought he'd better be cautious in approaching her. Probably getting hit on all the time, poor beautiful thing, he thought.

He introduced himself and gave her his card. Explaining the project and the need for a great deal of artwork, he asked if he could rent some paintings or if it would have to be purchased. She was polite and extremely interested. She thought she might need some legal advice if they contracted to use her work in a film. She struck him as very intelligent. They made arrangements to meet at her studio with his associate the following week. He would check with his accountant and bring the necessary legal papers so that she could have them checked by her lawyer.

As usual with small productions, the scene shifted. The producer brought in some art that he liked and decided that they didn't need to show more than a few pieces. Oscar showed up at Wanda's studio, a loft that she shared with a few artists, bought a few watercolors for himself and explained the frailty of film work. She was very understanding, a real peach, and he invited her to dinner at the Cliff House in Malibu.

It was memorable in that there was no sexual turn-on between them. He'd slept with a few aspiring actresses, everybody did in Hollywood, but he remained faithful, at heart, to his wife and their young son. He framed the pictures and put them in a place of honor in his office but never saw her again.

•••••••••

In the wan light of his Ashland living room, Oscar asked her if she could have coffee with him the next day. They had just settled into their seats at the coffee house when Kitty and Sarah spotted them.

CHAPTER FIVE

Kitty and Sarah walked slowly up Ashland Boulevard as they mused on the contemporary show they had seen at the Black Swan.

"It was certainly dramatic. Being right up close to the actors made the snakes seem all amazingly real. You don't suppose they were real, do you?"

Sarah laughed. "No, of course they couldn't be. But the way they moved in the churchgoers hands looked so creepy."

"That was a terrific play. One I'll not likely forget soon. It was interesting that the wife kept her husband's body so long, sort of had local meaning. I wonder if anyone watching it or in the play thought of that."

"Oh, you mean Stella's body laid out at her home. I don't think there's any connection. But the wife in the play did seem to keep the body a long time. They didn't exactly say but it could have been weeks. What do you think?"

"Oh, it was at least a week. And a good thing too with the mythological reincarnation. *The Handlers* was a very stirring play."

"I'll probably dream of snakes. Let's sleep late tomorrow."

"OK."

As they climbed the steps, they saw a small dark figure crouched inside the front window with what looked like binoculars in her hands. There was a rustling when Kitty unlocked the front door.

"Is that you, Mrs. Williams?" Though from the tiny shape she knew it couldn't be the portly Mrs. Williams who had attended each of their breakfasts for the past few days.

The figure stepped into the light and there was a tiny grey-haired lady in her early seventies, dressed all in black, with shifty downcast eyes. "I'm Jane Adams. Guess I haven't had a chance to meet you before."

"I'm glad to meet you," Kitty extended her hand. "We love your house and we certainly enjoy Mrs. Williams' breakfasts."

"Thank you. I try to keep the property presentable."

"The rose garden is lovely," Sarah interjected. "Do you do the gardening yourself?"

"Partly. I have a gardener twice a week, someone from the Lithia Park Service who moonlights."

"Well, it's lovely." The women chimed in together. "Well, good night," Kitty said as she turned to go up the stairs to the bedroom. There didn't seem much more to say to this strange little woman. But there was one thing that Kitty realized she was curious about.

"Mrs. Wiliams said you had a co-owner of the house, Do they help too?"

Jane Adams took in a short breath and waited a moment before she replied. "No. I paid her off long ago. I'm the sole owner now."

"And who was she?" Kitty asked curiously.

"It was Stella Jacobs. She had an interest in quite a few businesses in town, a few other Bed and Breakfasts." She turned on her heels and went into the kitchen.

Kitty and Sarah went up the stairs without saying a word. Once inside their room, they almost exploded.

"Stella Jacobs! Wow, another suspect," Kitty said. "What a strange lady."

"A lot of business owners would be suspect, if money was the motive. Is there some way to check which businesses she owned?" Sarah asked. She was getting into the murder theory also.

"My guess is she didn't keep formal records of it, bank mortgages, deeds of trust. Probably, she held some notes. With many part investments, she could have control over a lot of people in town. I don't know how they paid her, but if it was informal, she could save on her taxes. My bet is that the police won't find anything, if they ever look, and the co-owners will just say it was paid off. Like our unlikely landlady."

"Kitty, you're too cynical. Anybody that had business dealings with her would come forward. They would know that she had notes for loans and other records."

"If they thought she had records her husband would find, they would come forward, or maybe, as you say, they would just be honest."

"It's too confusing. Let's go to sleep."

In the morning, they questioned Mrs. Williams about Stella Jacobs as co-owner. Did she know?

"Yes, I knew she was part owner. I didn't mention it because I didn't think it was important. I just do my job. Jane's a good employer, almost a friend actually. I don't talk about her affairs. You're the only ones I really see in the morning to talk to. The couples in the other rooms don't even eat their breakfasts here. I don't know where they go."

Kitty could not contain her curiosity. "How long ago was Stella the part owner? Do you know when the mortgage was paid of?"

"I really don't know, actually. As I said I just do my job." Kitty had to accept this unhelpful information.

The meals had gotten pretty monotonous, muffins and fruit every morning. But they liked their morning beverages early and that hit the spot.

"Is the little Craft Fair still on in front of Lithia Creek on the weekend?" Kitty asked, changing the subject.

"Oh, yes. The booths are there most of the year until it gets too cold and the tourists don't come to Ashland."

"What is that?" Sarah was all ears. She loved craft fairs.

"Oh, I forgot to tell you about it. Some very attractive stuff. Would you like to go there before the afternoon bridge club? Oh, I forgot. I bought some backstage tour tickets for 10 am. It just takes an hour or so, you'll love it. We stop by the fair before bridge which starts at one today."

"I thought we were going to take it easy today. You're a whirlwind!"

"We have no plays tonight. So it is a day of rest from play-going. The backstage tours get you behind the curtain into the inner workings of the Shakespearean Theater."

•••••••••

Oscar took a sip of his coffee.

"I'm glad they have Fair Trade coffee here. It's very

big in Santa Monica. I thought we should chat since our progeny seem to be quite enamored. I love your mural, by the way. I knew it was yours the minute I walked in."

"Thank you, Oscar. I am proud of the mural. Since Brian and Juanita are both so young, I don't think we have to be concerned," she replied, stirring her coffee thoughtfully. There was a tension, a coolness between them. They didn't speak for another minute when Oscar broke the ice again.

"Being too young doesn't seem to matter that much these days," he mused.

"It didn't matter too much in my day either. I just don't want her to have to go through what I went through."

"I don't see how you can compare it. If I remember correctly your husband was a flake. Brian's a romantic to be sure, but he's an ambitious, talented young man, concerned about his future. Have you ever had trouble with Stella, any bad feelings, I mean, any trouble between our two houses?"

"No, I hardly knew Stella. I feel very badly that she died."

Oscar stared down at his cup. "I was so depressed the first few days, that I felt I could almost take my own life. When I was at my lowest I thought about Brian and decided to carry on."

"You must have loved her a great deal," Wanda said tenderly.

He waited a full minute before answering. "She was my support. She helped me become who I am. She was a very powerful woman and even though I couldn't come up here that much, and she hated L.A., we were in constant touch."

Wanda's compassion made her reach out and put her hand on his shoulder. "We'll try to help fill the gap, to ease the pain, Juanita and I."

"Yes I have such a small family. Brian is all I really have left. We should support their love, try to make it safe and comfortable for them."

"Yes, Oscar. We can do that."

●●●●●●●●●●

A large crowd of fifty or sixty filled the front seats of the Elizabethan Theater. After a long delay, Kitty was surprised to see Charles McWorther.

" Hello, everyone. Walt Dresden, who was your designated leader is laid up with the flu, really sick. So as a good friend, I'm pinch-hitting for him." He looked very handsome in a light suede jacket and jeans. He was very relaxed and gave a brief history of the building of the theatre. He told them they probably knew all about that and could learn more just by looking behind the stage.

Walking single file, everyone looked at the dressing rooms, the costume rooms, the green room that Charles explained was a place for actors to chill out. There were leaflets tacked on the walls from local events to out-of-town auditions. Beat-up brown couches lined the walls, which weren't even green. He explained the lighting system for cues. When the actors had to climb to the top levels of the multi-stage, they only had only one tiny light in the complete darkness before they went out on the stage.

Sarah was captivated by the costume room where the intricate outfits for all the plays were made. Some were re-made for the next season's plays but most of the costumes were unique and used just once, planned by the director, the artistic director and chief costume designer. Since Ashland was renowned for its wonderful costumes, this part of the tour got extensive coverage. Although most of the work was done in other buildings scattered throughout Ashland, the costumes for the current plays were hanging in different rooms.

As the crowd walked out of the main theater and across the street to the Black Swan, Kitty and Sarah found themselves walking next to Charles McWorther. Kitty couldn't help mentioning Stella's death.

"It was a shock to all her friends at the bridge club," Kitty added.

"She had friends? I didn't know that," Charles shot out. "It's probably mean to say that since you shouldn't speak ill of the dead."

"Do you know if she had an enemy that would want to kill her?"
Kitty asked.

"You think someone killed her? I thought it was her heart or something."

"It wasn't her heart. Have you been to see her. Her body is still at her home."

"You're kidding. In state at her home, just like a queen."

Kitty continued to probe, "We saw her confront you the other day. Do you know anyone who would hate her enough to kill her?"

"I didn't like her to be sure I know that Janet...hated her. She had made that clear all over town, but there must have been many others. She was not a well-liked lady."

"Janet doesn't seem like the type. Have you been to her Shakespeare Museum?"

"No, I've wanted to. Maybe I'll stop by. When is she open?"

"Every day I guess, though she wasn't there the day Stella died."

Kitty was almost panting as she trotted along with Charles as he swung ahead of the group, ready to welcome the crowd to the small theater.

"Just find a seat. I'll be in after everyone's seated," He called out two or three times.

Kitty waited beside him hoping to get his attention for more about his relationship with Stella, but he was too occupied with shepherding his flock. He regaled the audience with stories of the problems of such an intimate, small theater, and told them about plans for a new enlarged Black Swan as yet unnamed. They hoped to finish building in one year after the close of this season. He asked if the audience had any questions.

There were some technical questions, then someone asked about what it was like to live in a small town like Ashland, was it a stopping point for some actors or did they settle in.

"There are some, of course, who move on. Only a few to television or the movies. Shakespearean actors are a special breed and turn their nose up, even with much more money offered. Most love it here and have lived in

Ashland for years, especially some of the older actors. They'll probably be in productions every year until they die. For myself, it's my second year. At first I didn't like the small town atmosphere, but I'm just beginning to appreciate it. I'll probably stay on, if any director wants me. They hire from year to year, you know."

There was a chorus of compliments affirming everyone's belief that he'd return for sure. Charles looked quite pleased and, raising his hand in farewell, turned and quickly disappeared out the side door into the street.

"That was so interesting. He's a great guy, isn't he? If I were a little younger, I'd go for him. But I'll bet he's married," Sarah was smiling happily. "Oh, where is the craft fair, Kitty?"

Kitty roused herself from her thoughts of Charles McWorther's connection to Stella. Why did he implicate Janet? She pulled her thoughts back to her friend and, taking her arm, led her out the front entrance.

"It's just two blocks. It's behind the deli where we sat out on the deck."

"Great!" Sarah said as she toned down her walk to keep pace with Kitty's shorter stride.

There were lots of people milling around the attractively designed kiosks and stands that lined both sides of the cement walkway bordering Lithia Creek.

Jewelry, tye-dyed scarfs and wooden toys were attractively displayed.

" Look at these great bonsai plants and the charming pots to put them in. This is fine work."

"We can't bring the plants into California," Kitty said testily.

"We can ship them or give you a certificate. We do it all the time." The man at the booth must have heard her.

"That's good to know. We'll think about it."

They walked on for awhile, stoppng at a few counters, until they came to a booth with a jolly round man who was selling statues of Santa Claus. Each one was uniquly dressed, more like old St. Nicholas, holding a wooden staff or dragging a small tree. Most were about two feet high, with others three or even four feet.

"A little early for Christmas isn't it, Santa?" Kitty said pleasantly.

"I sculpt these all year round. Though I generally don't go to fairs since I have so many big department store orders. But I had a little stock ahead so I thought I'd try it."

The girls were intrigued and looked at each of the dozen figures he had balanced on boxes. He turned his attention to other lookers.

"Look at the faces," Sarah whispered. "They're all the same and they all look like him!"

Kitty laughed. "Well, he does look like Santa with those big rosy cheeks. They're great but so expensive," she complained while looking at the three hundred dollar tag on one of the small ones. "I'd love to buy one, but we better have a bite to eat and get over to the bridge club."

They picked up a hot dog at a stand near the entrance and walked over to the park, trying to keep the catsup from dripping down their fronts.

"These are very good, but I need some more coffee," Sarah said as they entered the club.

There was a subdued feeling in the room as they settled

at a table in the East-West position. The members were playing without much entusiasum, and the first table, with people who didn't even bother to give the girls their name, was very lackluster.

"It doesn't seem like they're having much fun," Sarah whispered.

"Well, let's just enjoy ourselves. Maybe we'll get some good hands. This game is so engrossing that everyone's mood will soon perk up.

She was right. The next table was more animated and the players welcomed the girls like old friends. On the second hand Kitty had sixteen points and opened 1NT. Sarah jumped to 3NT and it was passed out. South led a low spade. Sarah set out the dummy with eleven points but no long running suit. Kitty thought it might take a little luck.

Here is the deal:

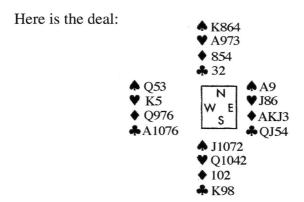

```
              ♠ K864
              ♥ A973
              ♦ 854
              ♣ 32
♠ Q53                    ♠ A9
♥ K5        ┌──────┐     ♥ J86
♦ Q976      │  N   │     ♦ AKJ3
♣ A1076     │W   E │     ♣ QJ54
            │  S   │
            └──────┘
              ♠ J1072
              ♥ Q1042
              ♦ 102
              ♣ K98
```

Kitty took the first trick in her hand and led the club jack, everyone playing low. She played three rounds of diamonds, and then played low club from her hand. She ducked and let North take the trick. North was end-played and led a heart to South's queen and Kitty's king. She cashed her ace of clubs, finally catching West's king so her last club was good. She led her last heart from the dummy. North took the ace, cashed the king of spades and a low spade. Kitty's queen was good. Losing only one spade, one heart and one club, making four, a top board.

"Well played," her opponents complemented. Kitty appreciated that coming from the thin mustached player who had psyched her on their first day at the club.

The third hand went quickly in a part score to North-South, and they all had a few minutes at the table before going to the next one.

"What do you think about Stella Jacobs' death." Kitty began non-committally.

"I think she was probably murdered by somebody. She had a lot of enemies." Larry replied.

"Really? Who?"

"Most of the people here didn't socialize with her much. She only played with her son. He seemed docile enough but still waters run deep you know. The members of the Board of the Festival didn't get along with her. And there were some actors who were really pissed when she vetoed their requests for spousal support."

"Which actors?"

"Charles McWorther for one. I forget the other," he replied.

Kitty noticed he didn't mention Janet Millhouse. She supposed that was because Janet was not well-known in Ashland.

"But her body is still at her house. Have the police talked to anyone?"

"Not that I know of," the player replied. "But this is a small tourist town. We don't have much crime here, let alone murders. I was really just spouting off. No idea what happened. Though we did go up to pay our respects. Didn't we Tim," speaking to his partner.

"We were curious. She looks quite peaceful, not like her normal hard-edged self," Tim answered.

The director stopped by with boards from the other table and heard the last part of the conversation.

"I heard that they were going to move her to the Funeral Home on Sunday. She's to be cremated, I believe. This would be the last chance for anyone to pay their respects. Better move to the next table. Your opponents are waiting for you."

Kitty was shocked by the conversation. Didn't anyone investigate murder in this town? She was deep in thought during the next table play and had to be reminded that it was her turn more than once.

"All this thinking is bad for your game!" Sarah complained.

"I'll concentrate now. I just can't get the picture of her body, so lifelike, out of my mind. Would you be upset if I asked you to walk up there with me after the game?"

"Well. It's none of our business. We hardly knew her."

"But I'm really interested in this case. I want to talk to Oscar Jacobs again to see if he will do something."

"It's quite a walk, but OK. We don't have anything else for the evening. I don't want you to go alone."

"Thank you so much, Sarah. You're a peach. I'll really concentrate now and count every card, so that I don't let any tricks slip by me."

•••••••••

The sun was still high in the Dresden blue sky as Kitty and Sarah climbed the hill behind Lithia Park. The sidewalk was tree shaded and an easy incline until the road reached the end of the Park and the women cut off to the right on a steeply inclined street.

Kitty was literally puffing as they neared the top and took the driveway up to the imposing, white Victorian.

"Let's just rest a minute, Sarah." Kitty leaned against the stone wall that bordered the drive. "I need to catch my breath. Not too good on hills."

"Well, now that we're here, what are you going to say?" Sarah's sharp face was folded into a frown.

"I'm not at all sure, but....oh, look at the back of the house!"

A shadowy figure was moving down the back garden toward the far end of the road. "We've seen that person before, Sarah. That monk-like figure in the Town Square."

"Oh yes, he'd been running down the Lithia Park Rd. into the Town Square. It is a he, isn't it?"

The monk had moved out of sight but the girls couldn't move a muscle.

"I think it's a man from the height and straightness, but it's hard to tell," Kitty admitted.

"We better tell them up at the house. That man could be up to no good. That's our entre."

Kitty knocked on the front door and, after a wait that almost convinced the girls to turn around and go back, Oscar opened the door.

"Oscar, I'm sorry to bother you. We were walking in the neighborhood. I'm Kitty Malone and this is Sarah Peterson. We met you the other day. We just saw a strange figure lurking behind your house. He went down that road, in a grey-brown monk-like outfit." Kitty was a little out of breath, with the steps and rapid explanation.

"Really!" Oscar stepped out and went to the edge of the garden where he could look down the road. "Yes, I can see a figure in the distance. How strange. I didn't hear anything in the house. I do remember you, of course. Perhaps we better look to see if he did any damage. Won't you come in."

They followed him through the large living room, past the bier where Stella's body was in full view, through the kitchen to the back porch. Oscar looked carefully at the area of the deck and went down the steps to the landscaping. He bent over in front of a large window that opened onto the living room.

"I can see some prints here in the soft earth around the berry plants."

Kitty could see that the dirt around the hydrangea bush was soft and a footprint was clear.

"You should call the police. They can make a cast of that print."

"What would be the point of that?" Oscar retorted. "It's just a peeping Tom. The house wasn't broken into. I'll just make sure the alarm system is on when I'm not there."

"But it might have something to do with the murder of your wife. Don't you want to know who did this to her?" Kitty couldn't contain her frustration with this seeming ostrich-like approach to the situation.

Oscar's handsome face looked troubled, ashen, and then after a brief moment, a certain lightness touched his features.

"Maybe he did have something to do with it. I thought it was .." he broke off in mid-sentence. "Look what you can see from this angle."

He was directly behind the footprint. When the girls looked over his shoulder, they could see Stella, lying immobile in the living room, beautiful, peaceful with a soft light falling on her face.

CHAPTER SIX

Oscar Jacobs, after graciously pouring a glass of wine to go with some cheese sticks that he served to them, made sure all the burglar alarms were in place. He then drove Kitty and Sarah down to the Town Square. They had protested that it was easier walking down hill and they really felt a need for the exercise, but he had cajoled them into his car in his forceful manner.

They didn't talk much in the car, just superficial small talk, but Kitty was glad that he said he was going to the police to tell them about the intruder. If the mortuary was coming on Sunday, then everything was being handled. "Finally," said Kitty speaking out loud.

"What's final?" Sarah asked They were walking toward their favorite deli on the Town Square.

"I'm just glad that Oscar is going to the police at last, and maybe this mystery can get solved. Who do you think he meant when he said, 'Oh, I thought it was done by...?"

"He didn't quite say that but I guess he must have thought it was his son. Maybe there's some history of problems between the son and mother."

"He couldn't have meant someone else. He doesn't know many people in Ashland."

Kitty wondered what the police were like in Ashland. She had such a good relationship with Mark Lipsky in Monterey that she regretted his being so far away.

"I wish Mark was here. This is quite a complicated case. So much more than meets the eye."

Sarah was intent on having a relaxing dinner, not talking about murder.

"What do you want to do tomorrow? Do we have any plays? I guess the theaters are closed on Monday."

It was hard for Kitty to concentrate on vacation time. But she pulled her thoughts back to the pleasures of Ashland.

"Sunday we have a play in the afternoon. On Monday, we could sun bathe in the morning in that private yard behind the house and then play bridge in the afternoon. There are movies at night."

"That sound great!," said Sarah, the erstwhile tourist.

•••••••••

Charles was feeling good, with Barbara safe in a hospital in Medford. He talked to her every day. She seemed to be getting along fine. He'd planned to spend the morning with her tomorrow and then all day on Monday, after his morning hearing, that is. He was curious about Janet Millhouse and her little Shakespearean Museum. What arrogance, he thought, coming to Ashland, the crown jewel of Shakespeare in America, and opening a museum in a rattletrap house. But he was interested enough to head that way after his stint with the tourists.

It took two seconds to get to the address on Second Street. It certainly is convenient, he thought and he liked the banners on the lawn. In this entrepreneurial country anyone can open any thing. There are no regulations in free enterprise except the monetary ones that would put a person out of business.

Well, more power to a cheeky woman, he thought as he glanced in the open door of the living room where Janet was dramatically describing The Winters Tale.

He listened quietly in the back of the room, admiring her self-assured gusto. She nodded to him with a flash of recognition but did not interrupt her talk. After about ten more minutes, she summed up with a tribute to women's rights which she felt was inherent in Shakespeare's depiction of women's virtue and constancy.

He waited while she displayed her cards and etchings on the plays, looking himself at her art work. He liked the brilliantly colored cards but the muted etchings left him cold, although they seemed even more Elizabethan.

She came over to stand in front of him when the last customers had paid for their purchases and left, standing just about to his chest.

"I've been meaning to come to visit your enterprise ever since I heard the bad buzz from Stella Jacobs. It's very interesting. In fact, I didn't think I would, but I like it a lot. Simple but meaningful." He gave her his most charming smile.

"Thank you, Charles. That's important to me coming from you. I've tried to get people from OSF to visit. You're the first one."

"Is all this artwork yours?"

"Yes, except that a friend of mine colors the cards."

"They're beautiful. We do have something in common."

"We both hated Stella Jacobs," answering her questioning glace.

"Not so much hated her. I just thought she was a bitch."

"I met someone who thinks she was murdered. What

do you think?" He added.

Janet's wide-open eyes showed surprise. "I thought it was some family thing, keeping her body in state up at that big house. Do you think it was murder?"

"I think it may be. When there are that many enemies, there are a lot of motives. She seemed to be healthy in an acid kind of way."

"Why did you hate her?" Janet was curious about this unusual man, so handsome and such a fine actor. She, of course, had seen all the plays and admired his work.

"It's a long story. My wife was working for her, some part-time social secretary work. Stella was terrible to her. Caused a lot of damage–a breakdown and panic attacks. I would prefer that you didn't mention that. I'm not sure why I told you. You just opened me up, I guess."

"I'm sorry. Is everything all right now? Would you like a cup of tea?"

"Yes, I would, thanks, and things are much better now."

Janet went to the back of the room and pulled the screen aside just enough for her to slip in to her kitchen. As she reached for the tea bags on the shelf above, she was surprised to see Charles behind her, pushing the screen back to expose the appliances and the sink.

"This is very compact. You've made the best use of space. What on earth is this?" His eyes were on a crude doll with strips of yellow thread on it's head.

"Just a toy from one of the children," Janet answered hastily as she slipped it in one of the drawers.

"Janet, are you one of the three sister from Macbeth. That thing had pins sticking out all over it." Charles was amused yet aghast.

"Don't be silly. It's just a child's toy. Why don't you go sit down. The tea will be ready in a minute," she said as she put on a stainless steel kettle.

"Of course," his tone was placating. "No one would believe it was an image of Stella anyway."

●●●●●●●●●●

Brian came around the bend of Lithia Creek to find Juanita sunbathing on a bench near their secret hideaway, her legs and arms exposed to the filtered light.

"I don't think that you'll get much of a tan here, darling. But you do look delightful." He gathered her in his arms, lifting her off her feet and crushing her mouth with his.

"I wasn't sure you'd be able to make it with your father here and all visitors coming to view your Mom." Juanita sweet face showed deep concern. She was a child in many ways, but with an adult compassion and a social maturity beyond her years.

"I haven't really seen him that much. I can't stand being in the house with her like...like that. I've been reading and writing at the library since it's so quiet and empty there. I mean the library at campus."

She put her arms around him and soothed his curly locks back with her right hand. They stayed like that for several moments before Brian broke free and, taking her hand, walked toward the door of the little stone house.

He reached for the knob and found that it was unlocked as it had been when he opened the lock with his pen knife, thinking that probably nobody ever came to this place. He brought her inside and found the burlap bags they had lain on their first time here, a time that in some ways seemed so long ago.

He had a soft comforter in a bag he had carried into the room and now he spread it over the bags to make a cozy corner. They were much more familiar with each other's bodies as they stretched out on his baby blue blanket. They took a long time undressing each other, the joy of anticipation was surging in both their bodies. He made sure he had put on protection just as he had the first time they were together. Then it had been more strenuous and perhaps a little painful for her though she never mentioned that. Now they turned and moved like a totally familiar couple and he kissed and touched her for a long time until he thought she was ready.

"I liked that much more today. I love you very much. You're a wonderful lover."

Brian's heart beat faster and he felt very confident of himself.

"I'm very careful to use protection so that nothing bad happens. But you might think about getting something for yourself." He felt shy discussing this very female choice with her but she really was so innocent, a virgin.

"Oh, I've already thought about that. I'm going to go on the pill. Someday I want to have a lot of children but not for quite a while."

"I want a lot too. Maybe four or five." He'd always wanted brothers and sisters and thought a family was the father, mother and lots of children.

"Well, at least two kids. That's the correct thing to do according to the ecologists. But if we have plenty of money when we're married, maybe we could have more. But I can wait because I think it was hard on my Mom having me when she was so young, though I'm glad cause she's sometimes more like a friend."

"Are you going to tell her about us?" He couldn't imagine telling Stella about his love. She was always very critical of any girlfriend he ever had. Juanita was telling him about her childhood, sharing some of her private thoughts, when he glazed across the room as the afternoon light slanted through the window and fell on the cabinets positioned on either side of the covered table.

"Look at that cabinet, Juanita." He could see it was partly opened. Raising to his feet and pulling her up next to him, he walked to the corner and opened the cabinet all the way, astounded to see the ugly bottles lined up. Some had a skull and crossbones on the paper wrapper.

"Darling, I wonder what we've stumbled into."

●●●●●●●●●●

Sarah opened the back door of the Hathaway Arms as Kitty followed close behind. They had seen a light in the front window and didn't want to disturb whoever was in the room.

"Maybe it's some of the other paying guests," Kitty suggested. So far they hadn't seen any of them, although they weren't in the house much themselves. They heard a low moan coming from the front room. Of course, Kitty could not contain her curiosity and her concern, saying, "Maybe we better go see..." as she crept toward the living room/parlor.

The bay window was covered in white lacy material, candle sconces on either side. Two over-stuffed wing chairs covered in flowered print on an off-white background were all that they could see as Kitty softly pushed open the oak paneled door. To the right of the window was a marbleized mantled fireplace with similar arm chairs and eight-foot couch making a cozy circle with a coffee table. No one seemed to be in the room. Then they heard another moan coming from the far corner behind the half opened door. There was Jane Adams on her knees on the floor with a picture in front of her.

"Mrs. Adams, are you all right?" Kitty came over to the half kneeling, half crouching body.

Jane Adams straightened her back and rose from her position on the floor.

"I'm sorry if I disturbed anyone. I didn't think anyone was here."

Kitty was genuinely concerned and came over to help this frail woman to her feet. She could see that the framed photo was of a person, but couldn't' see it clearly since Jane immediately hugged it to her chest.

"May we get you a glass of water or would you like a little of your sherry?" Sarah was as concerned as Kitty.

"I'm fine. Thanks for your concern. I'll just get something myself," and gathering a brown robe from the couch, she resolutely turned into the kitchen after leaving the tidy living room.

"How strange," Kitty commented as they moved up to

their front hall room. "Did you see who was in the picture?"

"I didn't see it at all. You were closer. Didn't you see?"

"Only a brief glance but it looked like a woman."

•••••••••••

Sarah and Kitty stopped by a Thai restaurant on the edge of Lithia Creek. Even though it was early, there was a long waiting list with reservations, since, of course, it was Saturday night. They went to a smaller Mexican restaurant off Main Street and were able to get a table right away.

"I'll have the Chicken Taco and the Chile Relleno, please," Kitty ordered. "A la carte, and we'll have a bottle of White Zinfandel for both of us."

"I'll have the Chicken Enchiladas on the dinner." Sarah seconded the idea of a bottle of wine. They found that they both liked the same wine. "Do you have Sutter Home Zinfandel?"

"I'm sorry, we don't carry California wine but we have something similar from Oregon."

The dinner was fine, and they were feeling good after sharing the bottle of wine. Actually, they couldn't quite finish it so they took it with them in a brown paper bag, not Sutter Home but a good Oregon wine with bouquet and flavor.

"I've heard about an unusual event that occurs in Ashland on the first Saturday of the full moon," Kitty said as she stood on the sidewalk outside the little Mexican Cafe Palomar. "I heard about it some time ago so I'm not sure if it still goes on, but it's supposed to be quite a blast."

"Sounds great! Let's go for it."

They walked through the Town Plaza and up the road toward Lithia Park. Instead of going on the path beside the twisting creek, they walked up the sidewalk until they reached the end of the parking area. Cutting across the last of the parking area, they followed the path behind the bandstand and through the more overgrown hanging trees and thick natural plantings of mountain laurel and ferns.

"It looks very deserted this far into the park, Kitty. It's a great way to walk off that excellent dinner but where are we going?"

"From what I heard it's way at the end of the park, wherever that is. We'll just have to keep going until it stops."

They walked for another fifteen quiet minutes enjoying the rough terrain and untrimmed trees, almost forest-like. Suddenly, there ahead in a small clearing, they saw shapes, people moving in silhouette, almost all in some kind of costume. They stood in the shadows watching in fascinated awe as a goats head passed close to them, past damsels in peasant dress, off-shouldered low bosomed, tiny waisted girls, boys in tights and doubloon shirts, jesters brilliant even in the soft moonlight in patchy strands of material–vermillion, orange, scarlet, violet, layered in a shirt of all colors. Many brought their dogs or maybe those figures were shorter people wearing dog's heads, costumes that could have come from the end of the year sales at the Visitors Center or made in the basement of some dark Victorian home.

There seemed, at first, to be no pattern in the movement of all these people, some dressed in ordinary clothes like Kitty and Sarah who had slowly, fascinatedly moved out of the shadows, but as they watched, the movement was in a circle that crisscrossed every other person in an intricate pattern that had half of the crowd was not moving with the flow but almost in an opposite direction but very slowly, a dirge with slow steps moving first in one direction and than changing to the opposite.

Kitty and Sarah followed the steps of the people who were pressing close to them, holding hands so that they didn't get separated. The sardine-like group that may not have numbered more than thirty costumed and uncostumed, moved slowly to the beat of a large bass drum in the center of the numinous, mysterious circle.

The drums stopped suddenly and after a short pause started a faster beat with sounds of other instruments flailing against the heavy beat of the drum. Small penny whistles, guitars, tambourines, cup drums and any sticks that could be banged together made a cacophony of sound as the circle broke into a faster rhythm and wider area. The loud noise and fast movement was such a contrast to the dirge that it took Kitty and Sarah by surprise. They almost broke out of the swirling groups. Still holding hands, they managed to join another circle that was not as costumed but just as noisy. Kitty jangled her keys while Sarah hit her comb against the bottle of wine. Soon they saw that the revelers were passing brown sacks and putting them to their mouth for a long sip. Alcohol was forbidden in the park, but no bottles were in evidence here and Kitty didn't think that a Park Ranger was anywhere near this group.

"This is amazing, Kitty. So out of this world. Let's have a swig of that Zinfandel."

"I don't think we'll find any of the Ashland Bridge Club in this group," Kitty said as she took a swallow of the bottle Sarah passed to her.

Sarah just guffawed.

In the circle closer to the center, most of the animal costumes were bunched together. Catching the full face of a horned goat as it careened by, Kitty was able to discern a unicorn and a number of dogfaced revelers passing the paper bags furiously between themselves, tipping back the masks to pour in their mouth whatever liquid was in the bottle. Then there was a brief empty space and a lone tall monk hopping wildly up and down, face hooded and cast in shadow but tall and strangely familiar.

"I think that our monk that just passed us," Kitty breathlessly whispered to Sarah.

Sarah turned around and, surveying the crowd carefully, replied, "I see at least three monks and one figure that looks like a nun except that her habit is up to her waist."

"To make it easier to run around the circle, I suppose. What do you say we drop out. I don't even want to see what happens after this bacchanal."

Sarah took her arm and they stepped under the cover of a large oak.

"Do you want to stay and watch from the shadows?" Sarah asked, panting a little. They could see quite a few had also dropped out of the frenetic dance.

"I'm bushed. We've had a busy day and don't forget we still have a long walk back to our Bed & Breakfast."

"You're right! Let's go."

They couldn't find the path but went through the trees in the general direction from which they had come and soon were able to hear the rushing water of the creek.

"There's the brook. The path must be close since it follows its course."

Soon they emerged near the road and shortened their hike back to the Hathaway Arms. Both of them sank into their soft beds after the briefest of ablutions and were immediately sound asleep.

••••••••••

Kitty rolled over on her back, her head still heavy with the images of her dream. She had been on the streets of an old Italian town watching young men in doublets and tights waving swords. She was not part of it, just watching, when the scene shifted to the dark morgue and the young man, Romeo. She knew it was Romeo lying on the stone floor. Above him there was a bier and a beautiful Juliet was dressed in white robes but the face was not Juliet but Stella Jacobs.

With the clarity of rational thought that the unconscious had brought to the surface in her dream, Kitty knew with absolute certainty that Stella was not dead but in some kind of drug induced trance. She jumped up and looked at her travel clock. My God, only 2 am. She would have to wait until morning. Maybe it would be all right to call at seven, lots of people are up at seven and the mortuary probably won't get there that early.

She was wide awake and suddenly very hungry. They hadn't brought anything up to the room from last night's dinner and they'd eaten all the snacks during the day. She put on her robe and slippers and quietly walked into the hall and down the stairs. There was a small night light in the downstairs hall for the late guests and she walked quietly into the kitchen. It was empty so she poured a glass of milk and took one of the plentiful muffins. Her mind was racing but she knew she had to be clearheaded as well as up early in the morning. The food calmed her down a bit and she began to feel sleepy again. Better not think about how this happened, she thought, just get back to sleep and save Stella in the morning.

●●●●●●●●●●

"Kitty, are you going to sleep past breakfast? I know it's Sunday but I don't think they serve after nine." Sarah was gently shaking Kitty's shoulder.

Kitty sat bolt upright. "What time is it? Oh, my God!" she exclaimed after looking at the clock. She raced into her jeans and shoes.

"Sarah, I have to go to the Jacobs'. I think there's been a huge mistake and Stella isn't dead at all."

"What do you mean? That's crazy."

"I don't have time to argue or explain it to you but I'm sure. I'll be back as soon as I can. Can you wait here?"

"Sure," Sarah said faintly.

It took only two minutes for Kitty to run downstairs and get the car turned around. The trip up to Oscar's only took five minutes and there she was knocking on this door at ten minutes past nine.

Oscar came right to the door.

"What is it?"

"The mortuary hasn't been here for Stella, have they?" She was breathless and very agitated.

"They left about fifteen minutes ago. Why?"

"I'm sure there's been a great mistake and Stella is only in a coma of some sort. She's not dead, Oscar. I'm going right now. Is it the Mortuary on Siskiyou?"

Oscar nodded and blurted out, "What are you saying? How can that be true?" But Kitty was already running down the walk toward her car.

●●●●●●●●●●

Siskiyou Boulevard was practically empty as Kitty's speedometer hit fifty. I'd like to pick up a cop, she thought. It could give me more authority, except it would take too long to explain the situation.

She turned into the main parking lot and saw the hearse in the back of a long brick building set at a lower level. She parked beside it and entered the back door where, she thought, they must bring in the bodies. Through a narrow dank corridor, she pushed open the doors along the hall. All the rooms were empty until she reached close to the end and there on the table was Stella Jacobs, beautiful in her serene state. A small grey-haired man was bent over a work table beside her.

Page 103

"You've come into the wrong place, Miss. I'll take you up to the reception area," politely spoken in the unctuous tones of most funeral attendants.

"No, I came to stop you," Kitty was practically yelling. "She's not dead, only in a transformed state. Please call the Medford Hospital. They will have experts on this drug-induced catonic state." Kitty only hoped they would have someone there who could analyze the situation.

"I'm sorry, my dear, your loved one is certainly with us in spirit but there is no breath of life in her."

"Look at her! It's been four or five days, and she still has naturally lifelike color."

"She looks very good. We may not need our cosmetologist to work on her." He gave a nod of satisfaction.

"She's alive, I'm sure of it. If you drain her blood, it will be killing her."

He leaned his balding grey head close to Stella's face.

"There's no discernible breath." He put his hand on her temple. "No discernible pulse, and she's quite cold." Finishing his quick diagnosis, he straightened up. "I have no authority to change the orders."

At that moment, there was a commotion in the hall and Oscar Jacobs came down the stairs with another attendant.

"Please stop your mortuary activity", he demanded.

"But,but," the mortician stammered. Oscar's authority overcame his work ethic and the hospital in Medford was summoned

"Thank God we were in time." He reached out to Kitty. "How did you know that she wasn't dead?"

"It's hard to explain. I've had a strong affinity to Ashland and the Shakespearian play here. *Romero and Juliet* had somehow entered my brain," she broke off. "It's really hard to explain but I just knew in my bones that she was alive."

Oscar expressed his appreciation a number of times while they waited for the ambulance to take her to the hospital. "I must admit that when you came to the house I thought you were too–what's the word, pushy, no assertive. Well, I'm so glad that you have that trait."

"Thank you, Oscar. I guess I have a lot of natural curiosity. Now we have to find out who did this to her and why they didn't just kill her instead of putting her in a comma."

"Well, that is the big question now,, isn't it." Their conversation was interrupted by the arrival of the ambulance and Stella was picked up and rushed to Medford.

•••••••••••.

The late afternoon sun shone through the Medford Hospital room as Stella opened her eyes and saw her husband and son on chairs beside her bed. She smiled widely and in a soft calm voice asked,

"Oscar what are you doing in town? You're looking wonderful." Her surroundings suddenly entered her consciousness. "But what am I doing here? Is this what I think it is?"

Both of her men came over to the bed to hold her hands.

"You're looking just wonderful! I'm afraid it is a hospital room, Stella. You were unconscious for a few days.

But we'll tell you more about that later. Now you just have to rest and get better."

"But I've never felt better in my life. I feel so rested, so calm somehow, as if everything is going to be just wonderful."

CHAPTER SEVEN

Charles came out of the Ashland Municipal Court with a smile on his face. It was just as the Inspector had said, a warning, suspended sentence before a warm and friendly judge. The police station was in the same complex, so he thought that he'd stop and thank Ardemis Grey. The way the city had handled his problem gave him a good feeling about Ashland. Now he thought he'd stay in Ashland and try to make a good life for Elizabeth and himself.

Ardemis was at his desk and anxious to talk. "How did the hearing go?"

"It went well. The judge was nice, gave me a suspended sentence. Elizabeth is doing well, on the road to recovery and I want to thank you for your help."

"It was the least I could do for one of our leading thespians. Did you hear about Stella Jacobs?"

"Yes, I heard. Some people think it was murder."

"No. She's alive in the hospital in Medford. Seems she was in a death-like coma. They saved her just in time. Gregory at the Mortuary called because it seemed so fishy to him, sending a corpse on to the hospital."

Charles had difficulty controlling his face muscles. It took all his acting technique to turn a bland face to the policeman.

"How did they find this out?' he asked softly.

"Seems some woman from Monterey figured it out. She and Oscar Jacobs burst into the Mortuary and took

Stella to the hospital. She's right as rain. Coming home today."

He spoke with a twang so that Charles thought he might be from the midwest, maybe Oklahoma.

"Will wonders never cease!" is all that Charles could muster.

"I'll have to investigate the circumstances. It could have been murder. It's important to talk to that woman, Kitty Malone."

"That shouldn't be hard, she's always underfoot. Well, thanks again, Inspector Grey. I have to get to the hospital myself now," and he spun abruptly and walked briskly from the office.

Ardemis Grey watched him with a bemused expression. How did he know Kitty Malone, he wondered.

He picked up the phone and dialed the Jacobs residence. Brian answered and explained that his father was out shopping with his mother. Stella was starving, she had said and couldn't wait to buy out a supermarket.

"Well, have him call me as soon as he gets back."

Ardemis leaned back in his swivel oak chair and put his hand together forming a tent or a praying position. He was of medium build, in his fifties, with dark hair and keen grey eyes. He had indeed been born in Oklahoma but left there many years ago for grunt police work until he came to Ashland twelve years ago. Not much happened that was criminal in this town. A few drunken brawls, fines for alcohol in the park but by in large, he ran a pretty smooth ship. This coma could only have been induced by some drug. He hoped there would still be some evidnce after thislong a delay. He was sure that straightlaced Stella would never had injected herself. He'd know her since she came to Ashland eight years ago when she railed into him for the parking tickets she was getting at that damn bridge club of hers. He'd worked it out so that a separate parking space for the club was set aside for a four hour maximum. And she still got tickets for overstaying that privilege. She was one difficult lady, but who would hate her enough to try to kill her.

The phone interrupted his thoughts.

"Inspector Grey? This is Oscar Jacobs. You wanted to talk to me?"

"Yes I did." His drawl was more pronounced when he had a difficult subject to handle. "You all going to be around for the next hour or so cause I wanted to come up and talk about what happened to Stella, Mrs. Jacobs."

Getting an affirmative answer, Inspector Grey grabbed the brown leather notebook, reserved for important cases, and drove his police car up to the top of Summit Street.

The house seemed remarkably open and friendly as if it had a personality that had expanded. Ardemis felt the warmth, the open windows, music playing from the living room, flowers everywhere, on the porch and the rooms filled with light.

He knocked at the open door. "Come in ," a voice trilled.

"Is that you, Stella?" It was hard for Inspector Grey to believe his eyes. There was a beautiful woman arranging even more flowers for the dining room table. "Well, I can see you're feeling much better. Any idea who did this to you?"

"Not a clue in the world," she answered.

"I wonder if the glass you drank from, before you went into the coma, is still around?"

A strained look came over her features, a glint of the old Stella. "I'm sure it's been washed by now. I've never done the cleaning."

"Is it possible to speak to the maid?"

•••••••••

Kitty and Sarah were sunbathing in the backyard of the Hathaway House, when a black and white with a City of Ashland logo pulled into the top of the driveway. Ardemis Grey went around to the front porch with its two white pillars framing a heavy door with a small cut glass window on top. A face peered out in answer to his ring. Mrs. William opened the door a crack, and behind her she could hear Kitty and Sarah scuttling up the stairs.

"I'll see if she's here." she answered his inquiries. "Do you want to come into the living room?"

He was comfortably settled when Kitty, newly dressed in her blue and white cotton gingham, came into the room.

"Are you Kitty Malone?"

"Yes. You're Inspector.....?"

"Grey. Ardemis Grey, mam. Oscar said that you had some information about the strange case of Stella Jacobs. Would you tell me all you know?"

Kitty didn't want to put on any airs about her detective work in Monterey and she didn't know much. She hoped she could learn something from the Inspector.

"I don't know much really. But I did think she'd been murdered and that the police should have been called much earlier."

"That's right, always best if there's a dead body. But how did you know she was alive?"

Kitty hesitated. Dreams didn't go over well with police, she surmised. "Well, it all had to do with Romeo and Juliet, I guess."

She broke off at his strange expression. "Well, actually, she never looked dead to me and I've seen dead people. There was color in her face. She was cold but soft, very lifelike. There's one suspicious character in all this. A monk that we've seen in the Town Square. He was looking through the window at Stella body as she lay on her bier."

She sat back with an air of satisfaction at producing a suspect, taking it out of the realm of dreams and intuition.

"When was this? Did you see him?"

"Yes, Sarah, my friend and I saw him looking in the window at the Jacobs house and, when we notified Oscar. He saw him too, running down the road."

"That's very helpful," he said making notes.

"Do you know who the monk is? We've seen him at the Town Center."

"We'll be able to check on that. Thank you for the information." He asked a few more questions and volunteered, "You are to be congratulated on saving the lady's life,the way I hear it from Oscar."

"Thank you. I was glad to help. What was the drug that was used on her?"

"The lab is still checking on a can we found at the house. Definitely something unusual, not your common arsenic or rat poison."

"Why would someone not just poison her? Why keep her alive in a coma?"

"Ah, that is the heart of the problem."

Ardemis Grey and Kitty were silent for a minute or two after that, both wrapped in their own thoughts. With a deep sigh, Inspector Grey bid good-bye to Kitty and returned to his office.

Kitty thought it was about time for her to make a list of all the suspects, those who might have benefited from Stella's death.

She opened her purse and took out her notebook. She wasn't sure about the alibis since she had barely questioned the suspects.

Oscar - alibi - not here
Brian - alibi - no known motive
Juanita - alibi together
Janet - no alibi - Janet was an enemy
Wanda - no alibi - no known motive
Charles McWorther - no alibi - hated Stella
Mrs. Williams - no alibi - no known motive
Jane Adams - no alibi - no motive except possibly mortgage
Members of the Bridge Club - no one stands out
Then there was the monk - no alibi - motive?

These were all the people she knew in town, but it could have been someone entirely different, maybe someone on the board of the Festival or some recipient of a loan. This is a lengthy and deffused list. She idly leafed through the notebook that she had found in the garbage and saw that a few pages were torn out in the back but the last few pages had numbers and word notations beside them. It looked like some strange code and didn't make any sense to her.

Suddenly the numbers and letters formed a pattern in her mind, one that she was familiar with. She knew these notations from her work on the Monterey Herald where precise locations in the paper were indicated.

This must mean something, she thought, but what papers are there in Ashland except the little ad-filled throwaways. It could only mean the Oregonian, the major paper most every one gets in Ashland. With a thrill of excitement she looked on the stand beside the dining table and picked up the daily paper.

She called the number listed on the masthead and asked where they had microfilm available of past issues.

She went upstairs to get her jacket and purse. She told Sarah that she would be back in a few hours, after some errands. Sarah was lying on her bed and looked a little surprised at not being included in the errands, but she was sleepy from the sun bathing and let it go.

●●●●●●●●●

Inspector Grey, after checking the records on drug arrests, came up with the monk's identity. The picture corresponded to his knowledge of a familiar town character, but as he read through the arrest report he shook his head in surprise. Well, you never know, he thought as he headed out the door for Lithia Park.

The afternoon sun shone through the mottled green

leaves of Lithia Park, as Ardemis Grey followed the path to the upper ponds. A figure with high hip boots and a tan park uniform was shovelling muck from the center of the pond. Ardemis stood for a moment watching before calling out, "Betty Jean, could I see you for a minute? Police business."

The figure tramped through the pond to stand in front of Ardemis.

"You can address me as B.J."

"We have you registered as Betty Jean Adams at the station. Is that your lawful name?"

"Yes. What do you want?"

"I need to have you open the lab storage building and I need to talk to you about the poisoning of Stella Jacobs."

"Do I need a lawyer?"

"I'm not arresting you. I just need to talk to you. You do have the keys, don't you?"

"I don't believe it's locked. It's been used a great deal lately," this said with a sardonic laugh. "Follow me."

With long strides, B.J.'s boots reached the stone building in just a few minutes and pushed open the door. "See, it's open to the elements."

Ardemis looked over the dank interior, the burlap bags, the closed cabinets and laboratory work area. He pulled open the two cabinet doors, and making a quick inventory of the jars and bottles, said "I'll have to take this is headquarters for analysis. Do you have any objection?"

"It's not mine. This belong to the Park Service."

"Oh yeah. What about this monk's cloak!"

"That's what I wear over my uniform when I go home."

"Would you tell me where you were on the afternoon of June 24th?"

"I was right here working on the upper pond problems."

"Did anyone see you?"

"Lots of people, but I don't know any of them. Is Stella Jacobs dead?"

"No, she's been resuscitated." Ardemis couldn't miss the look of great relief that spread over B.J.'s face. She had a big smile that showied her crooked teeth and lantern-like jaw.

"Why do you need to know where I was? She's not dead then."

"I need to question you about attempted murder¬a serious charge."

"I don't think I can help you there." B.J.'s tone was flat and non-committal.

"What were you doing looking in the window of the Jacobs home? We have a shoe print that will surely match yours." He looked down at the large muddy boots before him.

"I was just curious. There's no law against that is there?"

Ardemis didn't bother to answer seeing how uncooperative she was. She certainly didn't look like a she but they must have checked at the station when she was booked for possession during a sting at the Town Center. He was busy putting all the containers from the cabinets into the two burlap bags. When he had finished, he straightened up and turned to B.J.

"Please don't leave the county. We will be contacting you again after we've analyzed these materials."

•••••••••

Stella, smiling, opened the door for Kitty and Sarah, who were standing on the porch overlooking the Ashland Valley.

"Come in. Come right in. I'm so glad you were able to accept my invitation to lunch."

"Thank you for inviting us." Kitty said a little shyly. This woman with her bright shining face seemed so different from the tight, arrogant woman she had played bridge with just last week. "You certainly look well and different somehow."

"I guess I feel different. Kitty, I want to thank you for...for saving my life. As I understand it, it was a pretty close call. It's amazing to me that you knew I was just in deep sleep, I guess you'd call it. How did you know?"

"Well, intuition I guess. We'd just been to see *Romeo and Juliet* and I sort of connected you lying on that bier with her. It's hard to explain but I was convinced you were still alive."

"It's strange that you mention *Romeo and Juliet*, one of my favorites, because Oscar said he almost committed suicide himself when he saw me."

"Have you any idea who may have done this to you?"

"I haven't a clue."

"Well, I have some ideas but they haven't jelled yet," Kitty said diffidently.

"Let's not talk about it. I fixed a wonderful lunch. Please come onto the back porch where I have the table set up."

Kitty and Sarah followed her through the living room, which was awash in flowers, onto the back of the wraparound porch.

"Your flowers are beautiful. I don't think I've ever seen so many in one house. Oh, Stella, this view is magnificent," Sarah spoke up for the first time since their arrival.

"A lot of people sent flowers and then I couldn't resist buying twice again that many. I've just been feeling very happy."

"That must have been some drug. Do you feel all right otherwise?" Kitty was afraid it might have been some manic-depressive drug, but Stella seemed calm enough. They had a shrimp louis salad, very thin and delicious crepes and chocolate mousse for dessert.

"What a delicious meal, Stella," Kitty exclaimed enthusiastically. "I've just been wondering if anyone owed you money? You always have to look for the money motive, you know."

"Nothing that amounts to a lot. I hold a few mortgages and have a few loans out, but nothing that amounts to a great deal individually."

"Could you make a list of them? I've been involved in solving murders back in Monterey and I'm really interested in this case."

"Of course. It might take me a little while to make a thorough list, but I could get it to you. Is tomorrow all right?"

"That would be great. Inspector Grey said to get in touch if I thought of anything or have any ideas. I'll go over it with him if it seems relevant."

"What is your schedule tomorrow? I know you want to see all the plays," Stella asked.

"We'll be free after 3:30. We wanted to go to the bridge club again. Are you going to be playing?"

"Well, I will be if Brian is free. He's head over heels in love, you know."

"Yes, we've met Juanita. She's lovely," Sarah interjected.

Kitty didn't think the bridge club was the place to discuss the attempted murder suspects, so she arranged to meet Stella at the Hathaway Arms at four o'clock. She planned to have Ardemis Grey there as well.

•••••••••

Kitty was bubbling with excitement as she and Sarah entered the Ashland Bridge Club after an early lunch at their favorite deli. They got there early enough to see the crowd around Stella. Both she and Brian looked very happy and were smiling and taking congratulations from the regulars at the club. Finally at a little after twelve, the director rang the bell and the players moved to their seats opposite their partners.

"We have seven full tables. Welcome back to our miracle lady, Stella Jacobs!"

There was a burst of applause before they pulled their cards from the metal holders in front of them. Then there was a concentrated silence. Sarah and Kitty played in the middle range of scores for most of the games. There were no psychs, everyone being on his best behavior.

During one break, Sarah mentioned this to Kitty, "You know, there haven't been any psych bids since all this began with Stella. I think this club is a lot mellower that when we first came here."

"Yes, I agree. People are much nicer now."

On one of the last hands, Kitty and Sarah reached game while most tables stopped in three hearts.

Here is the hand: no one vulnerable.

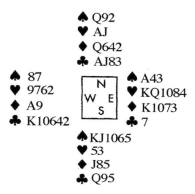

♠ Q92
♥ AJ
♦ Q642
♣ AJ83

♠ 87
♥ 9762
♦ A9
♣ K10642

♠ A43
♥ KQ1084
♦ K1073
♣ 7

♠ KJ1065
♥ 53
♦ J85
♣ Q95

Kitty saw she was going to lose two aces and possibly one spade and one diamond unless she could ruff in the dummy. Their opponents, a new couple to the girls who introduced themselves as Jean and Peter Griggs were bidding the big club so North opened one no-trump alerted as 13 to 15 points. Kitty, sitting East, bid a natural two hearts. Two spades from South brought a three-heart bid from Sarah. A three spade bid from North pushed Kitty to four hearts. Passed out.

South led fourth best spade taken by the queen. Kitty took the second spade with her ace and ruffed a spade in dummy. She led trump and North took the ace and led a low club. Peter said "Oh, I didn't mean to do that." But it was on the table and couldn't be retrieved. That was a plus for Kitty because she was able to take South's nine with her ten in dummy. She took the last trumps, cashed the diamond king and went over with a diamond to ruff out North's ace of clubs. She ruffed a diamond in the dummy and claimed, making five, a top board. They didn't wait to see the scores on the printout, but with so many things happening that day, Kitty wanted to make a few important calls.

"Let's get back to our room. I have some important things to do."

●●●●●●●

Kitty set the chairs in a semi-circle around the two easy chairs centered in the living room and, as the first visitor arrived, she said pleasantly, "Would you sit here by the door, Inspector. I expect a few more visitors and I think we may have a solution to why the poison stunned but didn't kill."

As Ardemis was poised to ask many more questions, the bell rang and Oscar and Stella came in together holding hands. She placed them next to the policeman and returned to her duties at the door. Charles McWhorther came in and, nodding pleasantly to Inspector Grey and briefly to the others, was placed opposite the Jacobs. There was no ring but when Kitty looked up she saw Jane Adams in the front hall.

"You said it was necessary for me to be here at four o'clock. Why are all these other people here?" she demanded of Kitty.

"Thank you for coming, Mrs. Adams. There are some important questions that we," she gave an inclusive nod to Inspector Grey, "would like you to answer. Won't you sit here?" Kitty directed her to a chair on the far side.

At that point Brian, Juanita and Wanda were brought into the room by Sarah, completing the circle.

"My friend, Janet Millhouse, will join us a little later, after an early tea. I think you all know each other and this is Ardemis Grey, Chief Inspector of the Ashland police. He will summarize the situation for you and then I have some important information for all of you. After that I will turn the discussion back over to the Inspector."

Ardemis cleared his throat and spoke softly and slowly with a slight drawl. "You're here because you're all in some way connected to the strange happenings that occurred in Ashland since last Wednesday. Someone poisoned Stella Jacobs that afternoon."

Just then the bell rang and Sarah, going to the door, brought in Janet,who was dressed in her Merlin gown of dark blue.

"I'm sorry I'm late. I had to stay to give rain checks for my afternoon tea and lecture." She gave a severe stare toward Stella Jacobs, who only nodded and smiled in return.

Inspector Grey acknowledged the interruption and continued, "There are a number of people in this town who may have had a reason to poison Mrs. Jacobs, and most of them are in this room right now. Kitty Malone has informed me of some investigation she has done so I am going to turn the discussion over to her at this point."

Kitty stood in the center of the semi-circle and pulled out some reprints of newspapers. "I have had these reprinted from old copies of the Oregonian, from two years back."

"But first, I want to go over the reason that so many of you are here. Most of you hold grudges against Stella.

You, Janet, because you felt she was blocking your acceptance to the Oregon Shakespeare Festival."

"She did speak against me at the Board meetings, of that I'm sure."

"I may have at the time, my dear. But I intend to visit your museum at my earliest opportunity," Stella interjected

"Well," said Janet with a gracious smile, "You'll be welcome anytime you visit."

"Wanda was concerned for her friend and for her daughter, who was in love with Stella's son." Kitty continued.

"No reason to harm her. I hope to be friends with her," Wanda answered.

"Of course, we can be friends for the sake of the young ones."
Stella was soothing all the old wounds.

"Now Charles is a different case. He had made his dislike very clear to everyone because of Board decisions which he blamed on Stella and because his wife had problems in Stella's employ."

Charles moved his feet and put a hand to his mouth. Stella had a sweet smile for that one too. "I'm sorry if you felt I was against the actors on the pension issue. I was wrong and I believe that went through anyway. I also apologize for my heavy hand with Elizabeth. She is a fine and sensitive person. I will help her in any way I can."

Charles' mouth dropped open and for once he had nothing to say.

"Mrs. Adams," Kitty continued. "You had a mortgage that Stella was pressing you on. But you also had feelings that were deeper and went further back. According to these papers and research that I have done, you had two children late in your life. Your son was oldest and the apple of your eye. Your daughter disappointed you when she became reclusive at an early age and moved from your house. She got a job with the Park Service, often dressed as a monk and is known as B.J."

There was a startled gasp from Wanda and a few other people. Kitty continued. "Your son, Tyrone, as I said, was your favorite. You sent him to college and he became a teacher right here in Ashland, teaching math and helping with the baseball games." Holding up some newspaper clippings, Kitty said, "two years ago, he was the referee of a game in which Brian Jacobs was playing. The baseball that Brian hit slammed into Tyrone's head, sending him to the hospital where he stayed in a coma for many months."

Everyone looked at Jane Adams, who had turned a dark shade of purple. "I sat with him for three months, every day," she began sobbing. "And then he died. I died myself that day. Nothing could take his place."

There was a stunned silence in the room.

"I'm sorry, Mrs. Adams, I must continue. Your daughter, Betty Jean, was a master gardener with a plot that Father Lawrence would envy." At this point Janet Millhouse could not hold back a loud exclamation.

"A Father Lawrence garden! Is that where the poison was brewed?"

"That's quite right, Janet. Betty Jean worked in her mother's garden and Jane asked her to provide a potion when the pressure of her grief became too strong for her.

After Stella demanded payment on the overdue mortgage, she snapped and put the drug in Stella's drink."

"I put it in a soda for Brian, after I found the garage door open. I wanted her to suffer the way I had with her son in a coma for months on end." She fell to the ground shaking with the huge sobs that Kitty had heard just two days before.

"B.J. didn't know what was going to happen to the potion that she brewed. She was trying to do what her mother wanted to get her approval, something that she must have been trying for all her life. That is why B.J. was at the window to see if the body showed any signs of life, after she realized how the potion she had given her mother had been used."

"You have it wrong. It was meant for Brian because with a stronger constitution he would have awakened in two or three days, but Stella is so little, it affected her in a stronger manner." Jane was fully cooperative now. "I didn't mean it for her, but I was afraid to come forward and warn them. I hadn't told Betty Jean about anything. I guess she guessed after I described the drug I needed.and how it was to work for only a few days."

"I wouldn't believe this if I read it in a book. A Father Lawrence garden indeed!" Janet exploded.

"I believe you are guilty of attempted murder, Mrs. Adams. I will have to arrest you on that charge." The Inspector moved over to the sobbing woman slumped in her chair.

"I really hope you don't have to do that, Ardemis. I can imagine how the poor woman felt," the new Stella interjected. "It was a terrible accident. I can see how it might have twisted her mind. I picked up the soda from Brian's room when I got home last Wednesday. I didn't feel like wine and I remember thinking that the bottle looked good. Do you have to charge her?"

"I can't charge her if you don't press charges, Stella. Are you going to drop the charges?"

"I think she needs some kind of therapy, grief therapy. Hopefully she can become closer to her daughter. Is that possible, Ardemis?

"What do you think, Oscar?"

"I agree with you, Stella. She clearly needs treatment. They have some wonderful doctors in Medford Hospital, I understand. Ardemis, we will not press charges."

There was a general feeling of bon hommie in the living room at Hathaway Arms. Stella even went over to Jane Adams and put her arms around the weeping woman.

Brian sat stupefied to think that his life had been the one in danger. The accident seemed so long ago when he was just in high school. It was hard for a young live-in-the-moment young man of the 21st century to connect with something that seemed so long ago. He was bitterly disturbed at the time. His ball just went in the wrong direction. He had liked Mr. Adams so much. They even closed the baseball games down for the rest of the year. He never went back to play, found it hard to remember the whole terrible accident now.

Juanita grabbed his hand, "How awful for you, Brian. It's a good thing that Kitty Malone was able to see that your mother was alive, or she surely would have been a goner."

"Yes, we have a lot to be thankful for. Have you noticed how much cooler my Mom is since her experience? I sure hope it lasts."

CHAPTER EIGHT

"What an exciting afternoon, Kitty!" Sarah was sitting on her twin bed. "You did a wonderful job! Do you think that everybody is going to live happily ever after?"

"I certainly hope so." Kitty felt absolutely drained by the experience. "We could take a little nap before we go to the Elizabethan Theater for As You Like It.

"Great idea," enjoined Sarah. They both curled up under their goose down comforters and were sound asleep in minutes.

●●●●●●●●●●

Dressed in warm slacks and carrying sweaters , mittens and hats, the women hurried down Main Street to get into the row of ticket holders going into the Elizabethan Theater.

"As You Like It is one of my absolute favorites. Is this the opening night?"

"Yes, It's the preview, which is a little cheaper for members. I think it's exciting to see it for the first official time. Let's get our cushions and blankets."

"Oh, there's Mrs. Williams in the booth for the cushions this time."

They walked over to her side of the long counter and waited until she recognized them.

"I do declare!" Mrs. Williams was pleased to see them, evidenced by her wide smile. "How are you this beautiful evening? You certainly did a wonderful job clearing

up the mess, the mystery. Jane seems so much more herself. I know she is more calm and contented. In fact she's
coming to the show tonight with her daughter!"

"That's great. You mean she is reconciled with her?"

"She always saw her but never accepted her sexual ori-
entation. I think that may have changed now. She may be
over the grief about her son."

"That's great to know. We better let you go on with
your work. Two pillows and two blankets, please."

"Here they are. They're on the house. You've done so
much for the Festival." She pushed away their money
and their protests.

As they moved out of the line with their blankets held
close to their breasts, they almost bumped into Stella and
Oscar.

"*Well met.* What a compact pillowcase," said Kitty, looking enviously at a striped combination pillow and lap robe
with carrying handle that they both carried. "Of course
you'd be here to see the preview."

"How nice to meet you here. We have the whole family," Stella said, turning to include Brian and Juanita,
dressed in light summer clothes, moving from the crowd
toward them.

"How much longer will you be in town?" asked Oscar
pleasantly.

"This is our last week. And what an exciting one it has
been."

"I hope you'll accept our invitation to dinner tomorrow
night, up at the house, unless you'd rather take them out
to dinner, darling," he turned to Stella.

"I do feel like celebrating. Let's take them to the new restaurant at the old Mark Anthony. I think it has a new name now," Stella interjected.

"That's a fine idea. You know where it is? Will six be all right?"

"There's the bell. We should go in. *The play's the thing.*" Sarah told the group.

"Wherein I'll catch the conscience of the king," Kitty whispered in Sarah's ear as they steered through the throng to their wooden seats.

They sat enthralled, immersed in the forest of Arden, and jumped up and applauded when the intermission lights went on.

"Let's get something to drink and see if we see anyone we know," Kitty urged Sarah. They did see someone and almost couldn't believe their eyes.

Jane Adams, looking quite elegant in a purple dress and lacy sweater, and holding the arm of a woman, was coming out of the seats a few rows behind them. They nodded to each other and when they had all reached the top of the outside lobby, Kitty said, "How are you, Mrs. Adams?"

"I'm fine, enjoying the play very much. This is my daughter, Betty Jean. Betty, these are the ladies from Monterey, Kitty Malone and Sarah Peters."

They all shook hands, assessing the tall thin woman with a long face and short hair, dressed in a dark pants suit with a white shirt and neck scarf.

"I've seen you before," Betty Jean announced, "at the Full Moon Dance last week."

"Well, that was quite a gathering. We couldn't stay. What happened after the dancing stopped?" asked Kitty curiously.

"Oh, after the drums stop, people just go home. My friend was there. Maybe you saw her, dressed as a nun?"

"Oh, yes, we saw her," Sarah volunteered, "It certainly looked like a lot of fun. We don't have much like that in Monterey."

"Maybe in Santa Cruz, but certainly not in Monterey," Kitty added.

"Well, it was nice to see you. Enjoy the rest of the play," said Jane, as she steered her daughter toward the rest rooms.

After they were out of sight, Kitty and Sarah broke out laughing.

"I guess we were caught crashing their pagan ritual or something."

They started to laugh even harder; in fact tears were coming to their eyes from laughing so much. As the laughter subsided, Kitty said seriously, "How wonderful to see them together in a festive occasion. Jane Adams looks so much better than the last we saw her, don't you think?"

"She looks ten years younger."

They each bought a pecan tart and started back to their seats.

••••••••••

Kitty and Sarah met the Jacobs in the lobby of the remodeled historical hotel, the only structure in town that was so tall, over five stories. The lobby had a huge tree

Page 130

more than two stories high in a giant pot. Balconies looked down on this central feature, and the walls were wainscoted in dark old English oak. The chairs and couch were large and attractively covered in bright flowers.

"This is certainly a beautiful lobby," Sarah said.

"This hotel has been here for a long time but is newly purchased and remodeled. We can wait here for a few minutes because we also expect the... Oh! Here they are," Stella exclaimed.

Charles and Elizabeth McWorther were coming in the front doors. Stella went to them in a welcoming gesture.

"Elizabeth, I'm so glad to see you again. I'm sorry that you were ill and I guess you heard all about me," she smiled depreciatingly.

Charles' handsome face held a warm and protective smile as he introduced his wife to the others in the party. After a few pleasantries, they all moved to a back room that served as the restaurant

"I understand that it's all buffet, so load up on whatever you want. We've reserved the large table in that corner. The room, while not large, was impressive in dark oak walls with a ridge of pewter plates on shelves around the entire room. The dark velvet drapes added to the medieval atmosphere of the place.

They feasted on roast duck and top sirloin with small browned potatoes and crisp fresh vegetables. The dessert table was not to be believed. The wine on the table was poured by the waitress and refilled whenever the glasses got a little empty.

"This is a real treat. Thank you so much. Something we will remembere whenever we think about Ashland. I hope that you will call us when you come to Monterey. We will take you out to a fresh fish dinner on Fisherman's Wharf that will be unforgettable as well."

Everyone congratulated Elizabeth on how well she looked and Stella asked if she would like to work for her again part time, since she planned to spend more time in L.A. when Oscar was working on a film.

"I'm going back to finish my degree at Oregon State and then I may study nursing. I find I have an affinity for the profession."

"A wonderful profession and one that is very much needed these days. More power to you Elizabeth," Oscar told the serious little face. Charles beamed, proud of his recovered wife.

"I wish I had a good quote from Shakespeare to thank you for the dinner and especially for making this such a memorable trip to Ashland. So I'll just say *all's well that ends well.*"

•••••••••

The next day, their last in town, they walked to Janet's Museum in time for the eleven o'clock lecture.

There were only two other people there and Janet welcomed them with open arms.

"I'm so glad you came over. I was afraid that you'd leave town without saying good-bye to me." She took down one of her larger etchings, a drawing of the Bard with dancers in Elizabethan costumes faintly in the background. "I would like to have you have this," she thrust it into Kitty's hand, "as a gift of appreciation."

"Thank you so much, Janet. You shouldn't give me such a grand gift. We want to buy some of your smaller cards so that we can frame them at home," Kitty told her. "Are you doing a lecture on *All's Well*?"

"No I don't do comedies. I was going to repeat my lecture on *Romeo and Juliet*, but we can talk about *King Lear* if you would like. That one is full of hidden intentions by Shakespeare because the continuing struggle between England and France gave every character, like the King of France and Duke of Burgundy, a deeper meaning. Would that suit you?"

"Oh, we'd love a lecture on *King Lear*."

"The Oregon Festival Committee called to ask me to their luncheon," Janet told them with a satisfied smile. "This is the first time I've been invited to anything like that. I think Stella is responsible. She has changed."

Kitty and Sarah gave her their congratulations and at the end of the lecture, took their remembrances of Ashland wrapped in brown paper up to the Hathaway Arms.

The next morning early, with their bags packed, Kitty said, "I hope our next trip to Santa Barbara for their Regional Tournament will be more relaxing, with no psychs, no murders, and no psych murders."